S0-AWO-432

If You Need Me

C. S. ADLER

Macmillan Publishing Company
New York
Collier Macmillan Publishers
London

With thanks to our veterinarian, Franklin Rapp, D.V.M., for sharing his expertise so generously.

Copyright © 1988 by C. S. Adler. All rights reserved. No part of this book may be reproduced or transmitted in any form or by any means, electronic or mechanical, including photocopying, recording, or by any information storage and retrieval system, without permission in writing from the Publisher. Macmillan Publishing Company, 866 Third Avenue, New York, NY 10022, Collier Macmillan Canada, Inc.

First Edition. Printed in the United States of America

10 9 8 7 6 5 4 3 2 1

The text of this book is set in 12 point Baskerville.

Library of Congress Cataloging-in-Publication Data
Adler, C. S. (Carole S.) If you need me / C.S. Adler. — 1st ed.   p.   cm. Summary: Having grown to accept and love her stepmother Dora, thirteen-year-old Lyn is increasingly worried as tension grows between Dora and her father and he begins to be attracted to her friend Brian's mother instead.
ISBN 0-02-700420-1
[1. Stepmothers—Fiction. 2. Fathers and daughters—Fiction. 3. Family problems—Fiction.]   I. Title. PZ7.A26145If 1988 [Fic]—dc19 87-36467 CIP AC

To Carole McLeod,
not only a superwoman, but a lovely friend

ONE

The sight of her father playing tennis with Mrs. Maclean brought Lyn up short. She stood behind the screen of bushes staring, while queasiness replaced the confidence that had filled her the second before. If she didn't live so far out in the country, she told herself, or if the late bus weren't so inconvenient, she wouldn't be chasing down her father to ask him for a ride home after swim team practice. Immediately, she knew she was putting the blame on the wrong things. The real reason that seeing her father play tennis with the lady next door could make her anxious was all those years when each of Dad's girlfriends had tried out for the role of mother. That was all it was, a reminder of painful times.

But he had married Dora. He'd been a married man for three years now, and it didn't matter how pretty Mrs. Maclean was, reaching for a backhand in her flippy little tennis skirt. Never mind her striking white hair and pink cheeks and perfect figure. Dad was married.

Except, just as Lyn took a breath to call out to him, Mrs. Maclean fell. Gallantly, Dad raced around the net and dropped to one knee beside her.

"I'm fine," Mrs. Maclean assured him. Her voice was the bright color of her cheeks. "I'm always taking tumbles going after balls I can't get." She offered him her hands like a gift.

He pulled her to her feet and then forgot to let go. For a minute they stood there talking quietly to each other, hand in hand. Brian's mother. Mrs. Maclean. Why was Dad so intent on her?

Lyn turned away. She couldn't stomach swim team practice now. Better to hurry and try to catch her bus. She ran from the tennis courts across the consolidated school district campus toward the low yellow-brick hulk where her father taught seventh-grade English and she attended eighth grade. Her bus was already pulling away from the curb, but the driver stopped and opened the door for her. She thanked him gratefully.

"No problem," he said.

No problem? Outside the window, blue sky gleamed above newly leafed-out trees as the bus lumbered past the tennis courts. There was Dad's friend Mark, the high school tennis coach, lugging a wire basket of balls onto the court Dad and Mrs. Maclean shared. Lyn sighed with relief. Of course. They were taking lessons. She was ashamed of what she'd imagined, especially considering Dad's strict standards of behavior. That and his teaching ability were what he prided himself on most. And why shouldn't he play tennis with his neighbor on public courts after school? Dora probably knew all about it. Everything was okay, Lyn told herself, wishing she hadn't missed out on swim practice.

The little third- or fourth-grade boy sitting next to her was eyeing her braid, which was as thick as his arm and long enough to sit on. Finally he asked, "How come you wear your hair like an Indian?"

"Because I like it that way."

"Indians aren't blond," the kid said.

"I'm not an Indian."

"Well, then, how come?" he insisted.

He wasn't being a smart aleck, just little-kid curious, Lyn saw, and she answered him honestly. "Because my mother wanted me to have a braid, and after she died my father wouldn't let me cut it. I've never not had a braid."

"Can I touch it?" the little boy asked. He reminded her of how her father looked in childhood photographs. With his long lashes and blue saucer eyes, Dad was still boyish and cute, except when he was being the stern-faced English teacher of the middle-school hallways.

"Sure," Lyn said.

Solemnly her seatmate fingered her silken rope. It had enough thickness and heft to hold any ship fast in a storm. "It's nice," he said, and turned to look out the window.

Lyn found Dora hosing down the inside cages of the boarding kennel she maintained behind their house.

"Did you know Dad was playing tennis after school today?" Lyn asked her dark-haired, wafer-thin stepmother.

"Umm, yes. He told me. With Mark, I think."

Lyn considered. Dad could have been waiting for Mark, and maybe Mrs. Maclean came along, and they were just hitting a few balls meanwhile. Sure, that was how it had been.

Dora hauled back on the long, heavy hose to move it to the next cage. Lyn bent to help her. "No, that's all right," Dora said. She had a thing about doing all the hard physical labor herself. She had hated being treated as if she were weak when she was a puny little kid, she'd told Lyn.

"So what's up with you?" Dora asked. "How's it going with the boy next door?"

"Brian?" Lyn smiled at the mention of Mrs. Maclean's son. "Well, this morning at the bus stop I got him to grunt."

"I guess that's progress."

"I don't know. From grunting to conversation could take years. Maybe it's not worth taking the bus to school every day just to work on Brian. I sure could get in a lot earlier riding with Dad."

Dora chuckled. "And fit in more extra activities that way, right? Is Brian the reason you didn't stay for swim practice?"

"Today I just wasn't in the mood," Lyn said. She'd been so upset by what she'd seen on the tennis court that she hadn't even noticed whether Brian was on the bus or not.

Dora was looking at her fondly. "I made some

pumpkin muffins that should be cooled by now," she said.

"You're the best." Lyn gave Dora a quick hug and headed for the kitchen. When they first became a family, Dora had stiffened in an embrace, but now she responded with the kind of gruff, easy affection she showed toward dogs. That was an achievement for Lyn. Dad accused Dora of loving dogs more than people, and Lyn always defended her, but the truth was she'd had to struggle for over a year to get close to the stepmother her father called his shy gypsy girl.

The swish of the hairbrush through Lyn's never-cut, wheat-colored hair made a counterpoint to the early morning traffic whooshing by on the county road outside her bedroom window. Pretty soon Brian Maclean would join the disorderly row of rural mailboxes where the school bus stopped. He always got there early. Was it possible he might be getting there early hoping she would, too? Possible, but not likely. She always had to be the first to speak, and he directed all his answers to the road as if he might give something away by meeting her eyes.

Lyn had had such hopes when she'd heard the house next door was being rented by a family with a thirteen-year-old boy. To have a friend her age within walking distance would be great, and his being a boy didn't matter. She'd always gotten along well with both sexes. But before Dora had finished baking a cake to welcome them to the neighborhood, Mr. Maclean had arrived to complain that barking dogs were keeping his wife awake all night.

"The agent didn't mention you had a kennel," he'd told Dora apologetically. "We didn't know when we signed the lease."

The noisy dogs had been picked up by their owners, and Mr. Maclean had come back, slump-shouldered and embarrassed, to complain only once since then. His wife had been just a flash of white hair whizzing by in a car to Lyn until yesterday at the tennis courts, but Brian looked promising right from the start. He was lean, with a ski-chute nose and freckles, a couple of inches shorter than Lyn. His best feature was his liquid brown eyes, promisingly crisscrossed with thoughts, none of which he'd shared so far.

The steps creaked under Dad's quick feet as he ran down for breakfast. How she missed the cozy morning chats they used to have in the days when he did her hair for her! Those heart-to-heart exchanges had stopped after he'd married Dora and Lyn had told him she could do her hair herself. He'd taken that as a sign of independence, but Lyn had only meant to step back from the place next to his heart to give Dora room there. Dora was his wife, after all, the one who'd remain with him after his daughter grew up and away. Wistfully, Lyn remembered how close she and Dad had once been.

She tied off the braid with a red rubber band to match her red shirt, then straightened out the frayed quilt that her mother had made. The room satisfied Lyn. It was neat and orderly, and everything in it, from the quilt to the unmatched tag-sale furniture that she'd chosen herself, had special meaning.

Her red flats made a racket on the stairs, but neither Dora nor Dad looked up when she entered the kitchen.

". . .Well, where would you rather go if you think the Outer Banks is too far?" Dad was asking Dora, who was huddled over her coffee cup so that her long, dark hair shielded her face. She often hid like that if she felt besieged.

"I don't know. It's just getting someone to take care of the dogs for two weeks," Dora said apologetically.

"In other words, you don't want to go anywhere. That's what you're saying, isn't it?" Dad asked. He never raised his voice. He used his eyes. One look from his blue-ice eyes could quell a classroom of unruly kids.

"I didn't say that," Dora protested.

"We stayed put Christmas week because that was your busiest time of the year, and now it's spring vacation. I think your kennel means more to you than we do."

Dora gave him a pleading look, then hid her eyes again. To help her, Lyn said, "Excuse me, Dad. I want to tell you I don't need a lift this morning, after all." Cinder, Dora's devoted stray, was scratching at the back door. Lyn let the small black pooch in while she babbled on. "I'm taking the bus. I got my Spirit Week Committee to agree to squeeze our meeting into homeroom instead of before school."

"Fine," Dad answered her absently.

Lyn thought of how he'd looked at Mrs. Maclean when he was holding her hands yesterday. He'd looked at Dora like that when they were first married, but not lately. Lately he seemed to pick on Dora a lot.

"Did you leave me any of those great pumpkin muffins Dora made yesterday, Dad?"

Impatiently, he pushed his straight brown hair off his forehead and asked Lyn, "What would *you* say to a vacation in the Outer Banks, honey?"

"Well . . . ." She was wary. "You know I love vacations, especially beach ones, but it would be fun to camp nearby, too, and then Dora could scoot home to check on things once in a while."

Dora lifted her head and flashed Lyn a grateful smile.

"We've done that," Dad said. "Am I the only one who craves variety?"

"The woods would be different in June. We went in August last year," Dora reminded him.

"Okay, okay." Dad stood and stacked his dirty dishes in the sink. "We'd better talk this out some other time or I'll be late for my faculty meeting. Incidentally, I've got a tennis game after school, Doe." He kissed Dora's bony forehead and said more kindly, "You try not to kill yourself over those dog boarders of yours, hear?"

A one-armed hug for Lyn, and he was off with the tie still hanging loose on his unbuttoned shirt. Dad wore ties and jackets because he thought male teachers should, he'd told Lyn, but she suspected he just liked looking nice. Looks mattered to him. Even in houses. For instance, he'd preferred a pretty Dutch colonial near the school to this rundown old farmhouse. They'd only bought the farmhouse because it had the kennel behind it. Owning a kennel had been Dora's dream, and back then Dad had been eager to please her.

Dora's face was hidden by her hair again, and Cinder had as usual crept onto her feet to insure that Dora couldn't leave her unexpectedly.

"Are you all right?" Lyn asked her stepmother.

"Fine," Dora murmured. She looked at Lyn and said, "Thanks," with a gratitude that covered more than the question.

Lyn found the pumpkin muffins. She had two for breakfast and refused to wonder who Dad's tennis partner was that afternoon.

TWO

Brian was poised on one leg in line with the mail-boxes when Lyn got there. As usual, he seemed to be deep in thought. "Hi," she said cheerfully. "Think it'll rain?"

"Someday for sure," he said, and let a grin leak out. The sky was cloudless. She always asked him if he thought it would rain. Repeat anything often enough and it becomes funny, Dad had once told her.

"So. Ready for the math test?" she asked.

He shrugged. "No, are you?"

"Well, I reviewed what she said to."

"Did you understand it?"

"No."

"That's what I mean," he said, and would have stood there in silence until the bus arrived if she'd let him.

A pickup truck slammed to a stop at the driveway of the antiques store fifty yards down the road. The big dog standing in the open back was shoved hard against the cab. "Did you see that?" Lyn cried. "That guy could have broken his dog's legs. What a jerk!"

The driver was a young man in jeans and a billed cap. He got out and opened the back gate of the truck. At his command the dog jumped down. It was a handsome animal, black with a white chest and face and tan markings over its eyes and on its cheeks, probably a combination of Labrador retriever and thick-haired malamute, and maybe some shepherd thrown in. Even from a distance, the man's command to sit and stay was obvious. Obediently, the big dog sat down on its haunches. It continued sitting as it watched the man swing back into his truck and drive away.

"I can't believe it," Lyn said. "He just left that dog there."

"Probably training him," Brian suggested uncertainly.

"Do you think so?" Lyn considered. "Maybe." Their bus arrived and Brian climbed aboard. Lyn followed more slowly, watching the dog over her shoulder. It hurt her to see the sturdy animal sitting so tensely, its head riveted in the direction in which its master had disappeared. She wished she could reassure it that it would be retrieved.

Her committee on Spirit Week assembled around Lyn's desk in homeroom. Spirit Week had been Lyn's idea last year, a way to raise school morale, which everybody had complained was too low. She'd heard about Spirit Week from a friend she still wrote to in Clifton Park, the last place she and her father had lived before he'd married Dora. The idea had been so successful, Lyn had been asked by the principal to organize it again for this year. So far the committee had agreed that Monday would be purple day, when everyone would come to school wearing something purple, and Tuesday would be hats day. Wednesday would be international day. Friday would be dress-up day.

Thursday was the only day they couldn't agree on. Ed wanted glasses as the theme, but Lyn's friend Shelly kept insisting on face painting. They'd rejected Lyn's suggestion that they make it both face painting and glasses.

"Let the class vote on it," Ed said. "That's the only fair way." No way was it fair. The boys would be likely to vote with Ed, and they outnumbered the girls in their homeroom.

"You're already outvoted by the committee," Shelly told him. "Jen doesn't care, and Lyn'll vote with me. Won't you, Lyn? Won't you?" Shelly urged, and added, "Because glasses is *boring*. So everybody'll show up in sunglasses and big deal."

"So what's great about face painting?" Ed demanded. "It's bad enough seeing girls glopped up in school every day."

Shelly glowered at him through her lavender eye shadow and pink lips. Her mouth opened for a retort just as Lyn noticed Jen's T-shirt, which said YUMMY. A T-shirt that said anything was uncharacteristic for Jen, who was a modest brown wren of a girl.

"How about a T-shirt slogan day for Thursday?" Lyn suggested.

They all looked at her for a silent minute until Ed nodded. "I'll go with that, yeah."

"Umm," Shelly said. "Not bad."

In social studies, Mr. Hoot was, as usual, wasting the period on one of his windy rambles off the subject when Brian called him to account on a fact about the Soviet Union. "Where'd you get that from?" Mr. Hoot wanted to know.

"From a book on Russia," Brian said.

"You a Communist?" Mr. Hoot asked.

"No," Brian said.

"Well, you bring in the book and show me," Mr. Hoot said, and smirked as if he'd won one. Then he beat a fast retreat to the subject they were supposed to be studying, amendments to the United States Constitution.

At the end of class, Lyn caught up with Brian as he slipped out the door with his books under his arm, alone as usual. She couldn't decide if he was the most self-contained person she'd ever met or the shyest. "Brian," she said, "you'd be better off not bringing in that book. Mr. Hoot gets nasty if you cross him."

"I can't stand that guy," Brian said with unexpected heat. "He's such an ignorant windbag."

"Right, but he's been here forever and he's the principal's buddy."

Brian shrugged. "What can he do to me?"

"Give you lower marks than you deserve. Lose your reports and say you never turned them in."

"Then I flunk his course. I don't care." He

grinned. "If I flunk social studies, my mother'll come charging in here and skin him alive."

"Your mother?"

"Mom's a tiger." He was still grinning as he moved off down the hall.

A tiger, Lyn thought. And what was Dora? Doe, Dad called her sometimes. Lyn shivered. Perhaps it hadn't been so lucky after all that the Macleans had moved in next door.

"Your braid's coming undone," Shelly said from behind Lyn. "Come in the girls' room and let me fix it."

Reluctantly, Lyn followed Shelly, who was already sashaying away from the class they were due to enter. Shelly's lack of interest in school caused Lyn to miss a lot of class time. Anything that didn't have to do with personal appearance bored Shelly, who wanted to be a cosmetologist. Still, she'd been Lyn's first friend here.

In the girls' room, Shelly laid out her own brush and comb as well as assorted clips and sprays on the counter by the wash basins and got to work contentedly.

"Sometimes I think you only like me for my hair," Lyn teased.

"Just wear it loose and I'm telling you, Brian will fall for you fast," Shelly said.

"I told you, I don't want Brian to fall for me—just to be friendly."

"I don't see why you bother. He's boring."

"Not to me. I think he's sort of interesting. Maybe."

14

"But not as cute as Boy Johnson. Not even as cute as *Ed*."

Boy Johnson was Shelly's current crush. Ed was last month's. Lyn knew better than to argue with her. "Start braiding," Lyn said, "or we'll miss the whole period."

Lyn couldn't believe it when she climbed off the school bus and saw the big dog still sitting where his master had left him that morning. "He can't have been here all day, can he?" she asked Brian, who was behind her.

"Looks as if he has." Brian sounded concerned.

Together they approached the dog. A few feet from him, Lyn started talking in a low, confident tone. "Hi, fella. Whatcha doing here? Didn't your master come back for you?" The dog turned his head to look at her with anxious brown eyes, but he didn't budge. "Good dog," she said. "I bet you're hungry and thirsty by now. I'm going to bring you some water." She offered her fist. The dog sniffed it perfunctorily, then wagged his tail. They stroked him, both at the same time, but his eyes returned to the street in the direction in which his master had disappeared.

"There's a tag on his collar," Lyn said. She probed the thick ruff of neck fur and parted it so she could read the tag. "Burlap. That must be his name. There's no license tag, but you can see where it was attached."

"That guy didn't want anybody tracking him down."

"How could he be so rotten! This is a beautiful dog."

"Yeah," Brian said, and squatted until he was practically nose-to-nose with the dog. Brown eyes stared into brown eyes. Gently, Brian rubbed behind the flipped-over ears.

"I just can't believe anybody'd tell a dog to stay and then abandon him," Lyn burst out. "Why didn't he take him to a pound, or better yet, advertise for another owner?" She was hot with anger.

"He's really thirsty," Brian said, as Burlap's tongue lolled out of his tender mouth.

"I'll get water," Lyn said, and asked Brian to stay with the dog until she returned.

The kitchen was empty when Lyn entered it. A strange car was in the driveway. Dora was probably taking in a dog to be boarded or returning one to its owner. Lyn found an empty quart-sized bowl on one of the open shelves in the old-fashioned pantry. She filled it and went back out. Burlap lapped the water up thirstily, then resumed his vigil.

"I'd take him home with me, but my mother's scared stiff of dogs," Brian said with regret. As if Burlap understood, he looked up at Brian trustingly and whined.

"I thought you said she was tough."

"Not about dogs."

"I'm sure Dora will let me take him in, but suppose his owner decides to come back for him after all?"

"We could leave a note on the telephone pole saying where he is."

"Right." Lyn promptly ran back to the house and wrote the note. She brought back Scotch tape and Cinder's leash, which had been hanging on the door, but it was undersized for Burlap. They couldn't make him budge when they tugged him by the leash. They tugged harder. He growled, an apologetic warning that nonetheless showed determination.

"Come on, fella. It's for your own good," Brian said, trying even harder. "Come on; let's go. You don't want to sit here all night, do you?"

Burlap lay down on the gravelly shoulder of the road with his head on his heavy white front paws and his eyes and ears alert to the direction in which his master had disappeared. Big as he was, in that position he was immovable.

"Let's try later," Brian suggested. "Maybe after he gets hungry enough, he'll come."

"After dinner?"

"Right. Meet you out here. When?"

"Around seven," she said. "I'll bring some food to tempt him with."

"No, let me bring the food. Please. I want to do something for him."

"Don't worry," Lyn assured him. "We can share him if you want."

Brian stared at her as if she'd finally managed to impress him. "You sure you want to do that?" he asked.

"Sure," she said.

"Well, I'd appreciate it," he said formally. "I mean, I've always wanted a dog, and this guy's perfect."

Impulsively, Brian knelt and hugged the dog's bulky body.

He has a good heart, Lyn thought, and she'd bet anything that sharing a dog would shortcut her way to it. "See you after dinner, Brian," she said, and went home to tell Dora about their prospective new family member.

THREE

By the time Lyn got back to the house, Dora was playing solitaire at the dining room table. Late afternoon shadows hovered behind her, and Cinder lay like a dark cushion over her narrow feet. Lyn found the dining room dreary. Its windows were shrouded by trees outside and curtained inside by the faded drapes left by previous owners, but Dora seemed to like it. She often chose to relax there before dinner by laying out a hand of solitaire, whiling away an hour the way her elderly invalid mother had.

Lyn had once asked Dora if her mother had ever played with her. "Never," Dora had said. She didn't like to talk about her childhood. Lyn imagined that it had been sad.

"Dora!" Lyn thumped into a chair. "Some idiot dumped a big, beautiful dog near the antiques store. Is it okay if I adopt him?"

"So long as he gets along with Cinder, it's okay with me. You better check with your father, though."

"Dad won't mind. Remember after my cat got

killed? He wanted to get me another pet then."

"You're sure the owner's not coming back?"

Lyn described what she'd seen. "Can you believe anybody would be so mean?"

"I can believe it."

"Would you look him over for me, Dora?"

"If your father says it's okay to keep him."

Lyn was pleased. Dora would be able to persuade the big dog to leave his station if tempting him with food didn't work. Dora had a way with dogs.

"Brian Maclean and I are going to share Burlap. That's his name. Brian's always wanted a dog, and his mother's scared of them."

The red queen Dora had been about to lay on the black king hung in her small, work-hardened hand. Tensely, she said, "Brian's parents sicced the sheriff on me again. I got another notice today that there've been complaints about the noise."

"Uh-oh," Lyn said.

"You'd think people would check out their neighbors before signing a lease."

"Well, the bushes are pretty high, and you don't have a sign out," Lyn said. She held her breath as Dora chewed her lip, considering the situation.

Lyn tried, "Maybe if Brian gets involved with us, they'll let up on you."

Dora laid the red queen down. "If they don't like my kennel, let them move." She added with a fierce childishness, "We were here first."

Lyn rested her chin on her folded arms and said soothingly, "Brian's nice. He really is. You'll like him."

"Maybe." Dora picked up the next card from the pile in front of her.

"You could look Burlap over now. I know Dad'll say yes."

"Now? I've got to get showered and dressed for that concert your father's taking me to tonight. He'll be ticked off if I still smell of dog when he gets home for dinner."

"You'll wear a skirt, won't you?" Lyn coaxed.

Last week Dora had put on jeans for the faculty party. Dad had looked her up and down and commented that the last time he'd seen her in a skirt had been when they met. Ruefully, he'd said, "You looked like a Romany princess in that patched velvet costume with your hair down." Dora had taken the hint and changed.

They had met at a folk festival three and a half years ago. Dora had played a dulcimer, and Dad had found her fascinating, deep and shy and soft and original. It was only lately that he'd been noticing negative things.

"Why should I wear a skirt?" Dora argued with Lyn. "Nobody dresses up for a folk concert."

"Don't you want to look nice for Dad?"

"Don't you start trying to make me over, too," Dora warned, and she smacked her cards together sharply.

"I'm sorry," Lyn said. "I didn't mean to make you mad. It's just—" It was just that Dad had looked so happy playing tennis with Brian's mother, but Lyn couldn't say that. "Come out and look at Burlap for a minute, huh?"

"He sounds like a one-man dog, anyway," Dora grumbled. "You might have to lock him in to keep him from taking off for home, and he's probably got bad habits."

"But if his master doesn't want him?"

"A puppy would do you much better."

"But Burlap needs me."

Dora looked at her and smiled wryly. Then she reached out and knuckled Lyn's cheek. "Sure," she said. "I should have known."

"Brian and I thought we'd try to tempt him here with food this evening?" Lyn made it a question.

"Food might work. If not, we'll think of something."

"I knew you'd help us." Lyn gave Dora a quick hug. "While you check Burlap out, I'll get dinner. That'll give you time to get dressed."

Dora said she'd have a bowl of the leftover home-made broccoli soup and the soup, plus last night's chicken, would do for Lyn and her father. Cinder rose with Dora, trembling and tail down, anticipating as always the moment of desertion.

Lyn accompanied Dora to the end of the driveway and called to the dog, who was still lying with his head on his paws, waiting. "Burlap! Burlap, come, boy." He got up on his haunches and turned his head to look back at her, but stayed put. She whistled and called again, but finally gave up and returned to the kitchen, while Dora crossed the road to keep her share of the bargain.

A few minutes later, Dora came back to the house

and reported, "Near as I can tell, he's in good shape."

Dad had already finished his meal, and Lyn was half-way through hers when Dora walked into the kitchen dressed in a long, loose, embroidered shift. Her dark hair flowed over her shoulders. "I'm sorry I'm late."

"Oh, how pretty you look. I never saw you in that dress before," Lyn said.

Dora's eyes went to her husband. He smiled as he looked her up and down. "Fetching," he said. "That's the caftan I bought you for Christmas, isn't it?"

It was, but Dora didn't answer. Without further ado, she served herself her soup and sat down to eat it. Dresses, Dora had once scoffed, were for Barbie-doll women. Lyn suspected Dora would put Brian's mother in that category.

"Dad says I can take Burlap in. I'm going out to him now," Lyn told Dora.

"Call me if you need me," Dora said.

Lyn put her uneaten chicken in a bowl in case Brian forgot to bring food. Dad walked outside with her.

"I noticed that dog as I drove past him," Dad said. "Noble-looking beast. It's nice that you're going to share him with Brian."

"Do you know Brian's mother very well?" Lyn asked as they crunched over the gravel driveway.

"Not very well, no. Why?"

"I saw you playing tennis with her."

"Oh, right. She's a good player."

"And very pretty," Lyn said.

"What's that supposed to mean?"

"Nothing. Caitlin was pretty, and the one before her, the lady executive. And right after Mother died, the one who was her friend. . . ."

"Lyn? Are you insinuating that there's a parallel?"

"No," Lyn said. "I'm sorry. . . . But Dora thought you were playing with your friend Mark."

"I did have a game with him, but I had the time wrong and Sylvia had a lesson with him first. As to Dora, she's pretty, too, and she happens to be my wife."

"Right. I'm sorry, Dad."

He squeezed her shoulder fondly. "You worry too much," he said. "Relax."

She felt reassured. It wasn't easy for her to call him to account. He didn't approve of children and parents behaving like friends. He said a parent's role, like a teacher's, was to guide and protect a child, not to pretend they were equals. He'd found that most kids who got in trouble didn't have an adult in authority at home.

Lyn stopped in dismay when she saw Brian standing beside the road with a bowl in his hands, looking into the distance. Burlap was gone. "What happened?" Lyn called.

"He just now took off. I don't think I scared him. He just decided to go."

"Probably on his way home," Dad said. "It's okay. Dogs have been known to find their way home over incredible distances."

"But what'll happen when he gets there, Dad?"

"That guy'll just dump him farther away," Brian said.

"We could catch up with him by car," Lyn said. "Dad?"

"Sorry. I've got a concert tonight. What about your folks, Brian?"

Brian shook his head. "My father's working, and my mother'd rather chase a snake than a big dog. She's got a dog phobia. Do you have a bike, Lyn?"

"A bike's too slow and it's getting dark," Dad said for her. He grunted. "Well, I guess I can afford a half hour. Come on. Let's get the car and we'll see if we can catch up with him."

Dora came out of the house just as they got to Dad's car. They all four climbed into the gleaming old Lincoln Continental that Dad treasured for its red leather upholstery and ample dimensions. He maintained it so well that the car didn't show its 100,000-plus miles. Brian and Lyn sat in the back, still carrying their food offerings.

"Let's hope he stuck to the road," Dad said.

Past the antiques store, they peered intently at every bush and tree and house. Lyn imagined Burlap hurrying home to a man who didn't want him, who'd left him waiting on a street corner all day without food or water. She clenched her teeth and looked harder.

"Now listen, kids," Dad said. "If we haven't found him in a couple of miles, I'm turning back. I've been looking forward to these Irish singers too much to miss them for a dog."

"Probably the guy just took Burlap one exit further on the highway from where he lives," Brian said, thinking out loud. "You know, to lose him. See, Exit Seventeen's back there, and if he wanted to get on the highway to go the other way, he'd enter it down this way, probably."

"It's possible," Dad said. "As good a theory as any. All right. We'll cover one exit on the highway. But that's it."

The road was dim in the graying evening, and no darker shape ran beside it, though Lyn's eyes kept searching for one.

Half a mile more, and they drove down a ramp onto the highway heading south. "It's a good thing there isn't much traffic," Lyn said, imagining the dog running through it. Dora hadn't said a word since she got in the car. She was concentrating on watching the road. Dad looked straight ahead down the gray gun barrel of two-lane highway that pierced the woods on either side of them. Brian's head swiveled from left to right. A few purple clouds had been left behind by the sunset in the slate-colored sky.

Suppose Burlap had taken a shortcut across country, Lyn suddenly thought. Suppose Brian was guessing wrong, and he hadn't even come this way. How could you figure out what a dog was going to do? It wasn't even possible to predict people's behavior sometimes, even someone as close to you as your own father.

She pictured Burlap arriving home with his tail waving joyfully to find the door shut against him. How much did it take to break a dog's spirit? Dora thought Cinder expected the worst of people because she'd been mistreated as a puppy. It would be terrible for Burlap to turn cringing and pathetic. Lyn yearned to prove to him that there were humans he could trust.

Brian swallowed audibly and muttered, "I don't see him."

"There's the sign for the next exit," Dad said. "One mile. He mustn't have come this way, Brian."

"Maybe not," Brian admitted.

"But he has to be somewhere," Lyn said. She would not let them give up. She would not. An instant later she yelled, "There he is!"

Burlap was passing a billboard, loping steadily along the margin of the road ahead of them, but on the other side.

"Hang on, everyone," Dad said. He drove past the dog, waited for a truck to pass, and made a U turn. When he pulled off on the shoulder, Brian and Lyn hopped out together and began calling.

"Burlap, here, Burlap. Good boy. Come on, Burlap. Here, boy."

The dog looked up and swerved into the road to get around them. Lyn screamed as a car speeding past clipped his side and kept going without even slowing down. Burlap had been hurled across the lane back onto the shoulder. He lay there, ominously still. They ran in slow motion to his side.

"We killed him," Lyn whispered. She pressed her knuckles into her lips to keep from screaming.

Gently Dora probed the thick black hair on his back and then the white chest and belly hair. "He's alive. He's in shock now, but his heart's still beating. We'd better get him to a vet."

"I've got a tarp in the back that we can ease him onto so we can carry him," Dad said.

"Don't worry about the vet bills," Brian offered. "I've got money from doing yard work last year, more than a hundred dollars, and I can earn more."

At Dad's suggestion, Brian called his mother to tell her where they were as soon as they got to the vet's office.

"What did she say?" Dad asked when Brian returned to the bench in the waiting room.

"Not much," Brian said. "She wanted to know where Burlap was going to live, and I told her your house." He grinned. "She thinks I lucked out to be sharing a dog. It's the only way I'd ever get to keep one."

The concert was over by the time they'd finished waiting for the doctor, who said Burlap would be fine but should stay overnight for observation and X rays. The vet suspected a fractured pelvis.

As Dad was driving them home, Lyn leaned over the backseat and kissed his ear. "You're a wonderful father," she said. "I'm sorry about the concert."

"Me, too," Dad admitted. "Well, it was missed in a good cause, but you had better be ready for nursing duty when we get your dog home."

"Lyn and I can handle it. It'll be easy with two of us," Brian said. He flashed a warm smile at Lyn.

Their friendship was a sure thing now, she thought gladly. She wouldn't have to depend on catching him at the bus stop to talk anymore.

"And," Brian joked, "anytime my mom gives me a hard time, I can threaten to move Burlap to our house."

"He's a good kid," Dad remarked later, after Brian had disappeared into the shrubbery, heading home. "Looks as if the Macleans may turn out to be fine neighbors, after all."

"They complained about the noise from the kennel again," Dora said.

"Did they? Well, maybe that'll stop now that Brian's part owner of a dog over here."

"I don't know what that woman wants from me," Dora said. "If she can't stand dogs, she ought to move."

"Phobias aren't something people can help, Dora," Dad said.

"I don't like people who don't like animals," Dora said grimly.

Dad raised his eyebrows. Lyn recognized the onset of a put-down and said quickly, "Oh, Dora, your new dress! I'll bet it's full of dog hair and saliva."

"It'll wash," Dora said.

"And I'm sorry you didn't get to the concert."

"No matter."

"Dora didn't care whether she went or not," Dad said. He unlocked the back door and held it for them to enter.

Dora stopped short and asked him, "Why do you say that?"

"Well, you didn't show much enthusiasm when I got the tickets."

"I never show much enthusiasm," Dora said.

"Except for dogs." His smile didn't take the edge off the remark.

That night Lyn slept restlessly. Her dreams were peopled with long-ago women friends of her father's, like the flighty Caitlin, whose debts Dad had helped to pay, and the stiff-faced lady executive who had called Lyn Pocahontas because of her braid and suggested that Dad give up the teaching he loved for a job that paid a decent wage. The one Lyn had had the easiest time calling "Mother" in her thoughts was the first one, her mother's friend Jane, but Dad had gotten tired of her. He liked interesting women.

Dora was interesting, different. It had taken Lyn two years before she'd dared to try calling Dora "Mother." The first time she'd done it, Dora had said quickly, "Just keep calling me by my name." She hadn't meant to be mean, Lyn had decided. Probably Dora wasn't comfortable with the image of herself as "Mother" to a half-grown child. But she was coming closer to accepting it. At least, judging by the loving way Dora treated her, Lyn believed she was.

Once Lyn startled herself into wakefulness and sat bolt upright to stare into the dark. Why was she so agitated when she'd gotten everything she wanted, boy and dog both? Burlap would get well. Dad liked Brian. Everything was fine. Still, she sat there a long time staring out at a patch of star-trimmed dark and listening to the wind, which seemed to be trying to shush her fears.

FOUR

Lyn bounced out of bed with her usual early morning energy and immediately went digging through her closet for her old, discarded sleeping bag to make a bed for Burlap near her own. She was folding the bag into a cushion between the high-legged dresser and the window, when she suddenly realized that he wasn't going to climb stairs too easily if he did have a fractured pelvis. The kitchen would be better for him until he was well.

She ran downstairs to call the vet's for a report. Dora stood at the back door, poised to go out, while Dad sat at the kitchen table, talking to her earnestly about how they should entertain more.

"Good morning, you two," Lyn said, and picked up the phone. Dogs were variously yipping, yowling or barking for their breakfast in the distance. No doubt Dora was late with their morning feeding.

The receptionist at the animal hospital put Lyn on hold and filled her right ear with sentimental music.

Dad stopped talking. Dora was still clutching the doorknob.

"Could you lend me a feeding bowl and one for water for Burlap?" Lyn thought to ask her.

"Sure," Dora said. Abruptly she opened the door and made her escape.

Dad had an English muffin in one hand and a red pen in the other, poised over the English compositions he was marking. "Is Dora upset about something?" Lyn asked him.

Instead of answering, Dad said, "Tell me, don't you think it would be neighborly to invite your friend Brian and his parents over for supper some evening?"

Lyn considered while the dance music percolated in her ear. "I suppose so. Except, Dad, they've been so nasty to Dora about the kennel. Why should she have to entertain them?"

"If they got to know us, they might be more tolerant of Dora's dog boarders. We could disarm the enemy with charm."

"You mean disarm *her*," Lyn said. "Mrs. Maclean's the problem."

The vet came on the line just then. Lyn asked about Burlap and was told they could pick him up that evening. Dad agreed to take her when she relayed the good news. "You playing tennis again this afternoon?" she asked.

"I might. The weather's perfect for it."

"Good. Then I can get a ride home with you. I've got to make up swim practice and the pool should be free today. I bet my timing's terrible. I bet I can't do my forty laps."

"It wouldn't kill Dora to entertain the Macleans," Dad mumbled to himself.

If he wasn't that taken by Mrs. Maclean, why was he so fixated on the family, Lyn wondered. But he had told her she had nothing to worry about, and she wasn't going to waste her time worrying over nothing.

That morning Brian spoke to her first at the bus stop. "I checked with the vet. Burlap's doing fine."

"I know. I called, too."

Brian grinned. "We ought to get together on who's responsible for what. Which reminds me, I'll get his license."

"Oh, right. We need one, don't we? Tell you what. You take charge of flea powders and bad-breath control and licenses, and I'll feed him."

He laughed. "And poop scooping's my job, too, right?"

"Right." More seriously, she added, "There should be plenty for us both to do for him."

"Okay," Brian said. "We'll play it by ear if you want, but the thing is, he's living at your house, not mine. So you've got the advantage, and I want him to know he's my dog, too. I mean—"

"I know what you mean. . . . You really wanted a dog bad, didn't you?"

"Yeah." With some embarrassment, he confided, "When I was a little kid, I had an imaginary dog, a big guy like Burlap, who always defended me. See, I got picked on a lot by the other kids until my dad took me to self-defense classes for peewees."

Now that they were partners, he was going to trust her with his secrets, Lyn thought, glad that he was finally opening up. She took a deep breath and plunged into their new relationship by asking, "Why's your mother so scared of dogs, Brian?"

"She just says 'bad childhood experiences' and won't talk about it, but actually, Mom's not much of an animal lover. She's always showing Dad and me articles about how pets carry disease or turn on people. My dad got me a pair of gerbils once." Brian chuckled. "Those gerbils should have been in the *Guinness Book of World Records* for baby production. We ran out of kids to give them away to before the parents finally died." He shrugged. His characteristic comment on life, Lyn noted.

The bus's square yellow head was coming toward them. "Want to go along this evening to pick up *our* dog?" she asked. Brian agreed eagerly. He even sat down next to her on the bus, another first.

"Maclean is a Scotch name, isn't it?" she asked him. He nodded. "If you had a kilt, you could wear it on international day."

"What's that?"

"Haven't you seen the posters around the school for Spirit Week? It's the last week of May, and international day is part of it."

"Oh, yeah. I don't much go for that kind of stuff."

"Brian! That's my special project. You've *got* to participate. Last year everybody but the real deadbeats did."

He frowned. "Do you get to boss me around because we share a dog?"

Being bossy and her braid were the two subjects Lyn minded being teased about. "It's not bossiness to make suggestions to people for their own good," she said.

"You sounded like you were giving me an order, not a suggestion."

She looked out the window. She did have a tendency to take charge, and some people resented that. It was all in the way you put things, Dad had told her. She just came on too strong sometimes.

Brian's eyes were big with dismay as he touched her arm to get her attention. "I didn't mean to hurt your feelings," he said. "Actually, you're right. My mother's after me to participate more, too, and I will, once I get used to it here. Hey, Dutchy, don't be mad at me."

She had to laugh. In backing off one sore spot, he'd landed right on the other. "Brian," she said. "I like my braid, but I hate the nicknames that go with it."

"Okay, okay. I'm sorry." He looked at her uneasily. They'd had their first fight, and they'd just barely become friends.

The bus had reached the city limits. In another minute they'd be at school. Lyn stroked the braid flipped over her shoulder as if it were a silky pet. Back came her mother's blossomy scent and the soothing whisper of the hairbrush. Often enough, Lyn had wished her hair were shorter and easier to care for. Then she wouldn't have to wash it in the evening and let the long wet length of it dry in bed overnight, because a hair dryer was too tedious. Sometimes she'd admire a hairstyle and wonder how it would look on her, but the braid was who she was. She couldn't cut it.

"May I still go get Burlap with you?" Brian asked as they climbed off the bus.

"Sure." She smiled at him to show she wasn't angry.

In first-period science, Jen passed her a note. "You know why Shelly stayed home? Boy Johnson circulated her love note to him, and his friends laughed at her about it in the mall last night."

"I'll call her," Lyn wrote back.

She was stopped in the hall by a girl with a message from Shelly that she wanted Lyn to come to her house after school. "She said it was urgent," the girl reported.

Lyn nodded, not too alarmed. All Shelly's feelings were urgent because while she had them she could never imagine they would change or end. Nevertheless, Lyn headed for the office to give her a call before lunch.

Suddenly, Boy Johnson leaped in front of her. "Halt! I've gotta tell you, I can't do the pitch to the faculty meeting Friday, Lyn. The coach says anyone who doesn't show up Friday morning is off the team."

"But didn't you tell him how important this is?"

"He says anybody can talk to teachers, but who's got the legs for the hurdles like me?"

"He won't put you off the team, Boy."

"Want to bet? He'd do it just to show how tough he is."

Lyn groaned. Boy Johnson not only had long legs, but he could talk people into anything, and the teachers all loved him. Well, they liked her, too. She'd go herself and give the pitch. She'd just tell them they had a duty as developers of youth to participate in Spirit Week wholeheartedly by dressing up according to the requirements of the day. Some of them, especially the older ones, hated making fools of themselves as much as the kids did. But being foolish helped break down barriers between people and made Spirit Week successful. She'd better try to explain that, too.

"Why'd you do that to Shelly?" Lyn asked Boy Johnson sharply.

"Do what?" His expression was one of exaggerated innocence.

"Show your friends what she wrote you."

He sighed. "Listen, Lyn, that friend of yours is a fruitcake, and I don't want her getting ideas about me."

"You mean the great Boy Johnson couldn't possibly be interested in her?"

"Come on," he said. "I didn't do anything so bad."

Nobody answered the phone at Shelly's house. Lyn figured she had better skip swim practice again and go give Shelly some support. Boy Johnson wasn't the only one in danger of being dropped from a team.

Three o'clock came, and Lyn told her father she didn't need a ride after all. Then she hiked the half-mile across town to Shelly's house, which was backed up to a gas station. The door opened and Shelly flung her arms around Lyn.

"I've been crying all day," Shelly said.

"Why didn't you answer the phone?"

"I don't know. I slept some, I guess." She looked pale. Crying made Lyn look red and puffy, but Shelly looked prettier, maybe because the tears had washed off the makeup.

"They've already forgotten your note," Lyn said.

"You heard about it?"

"Jen told me."

"Oh, Jen! That cold fish. I don't understand what you see in her."

Lyn knew better than to take Shelly's criticism of Jen at face value. Shelly didn't like anybody who threatened her closeness to Lyn. "Did Jen say something you didn't like?" Lyn asked.

"She says Boy's too conceited to like anybody but himself."

"Well, that's true, isn't it? Anyway, Shell, I wish you'd get a crush on somebody who likes you back for a change."

"There isn't anybody," Shelly wailed. "Look at me. I'm stupid and ugly. Who'd like me? Do you like me, Lyn? Really? Are you really my best friend?"

"You know I am." Lyn hugged her.

"Then why doesn't *he* like me?" Shelly asked, returning to Boy Johnson.

"Forget him. There are ten other boys you could melt with a smile."

"Name one."

Dutifully, Lyn began naming boys while Shelly alternated between sounds of disgust and negative remarks. Dealing with Shelly in a mood like this was more exhausting than swimming laps any day, Lyn decided. She finally told Shelly about Burlap and Brian to get her interested in something besides herself. It seemed to work.

". . . And so are you going to school tomorrow?" Lyn asked.

"You think they'll give me a hard time about that note?"

"If anybody does, I'll make them sorry," Lyn promised.

"I'm so lucky you're my friend." Shelly's tears glistened prettily.

Her mother arrived home from work then. As emotional as her daughter, she grabbed Lyn's hands and held tight while she expressed her joy at finding Lyn there. "You're *such* a good influence on her, Lyn. I'm *so* glad you're her friend."

Finally Lyn disentangled herself, and Shelly's mother drove her home. "She really has to go to school tomorrow," Lyn said.

"Don't you worry. I'll *make* her go," Shelly's mother said. She went on about it for so long that Lyn felt like some kind of attendance officer.

Dinner was emitting warm aromas of tomato and spicy beef when Lyn walked in. Dora looked up and said, "I thought you were coming home with your father."

"Isn't he here yet? Maybe he's still playing tennis. I

didn't swim. I had to help Shelly through a crisis."

"Another one?" Dora shook her head. "Brian called to find out what time you're leaving for the vet's."

It was six o'clock. Tennis had never made Dad this late. "I hope Dad didn't have an accident or something," Lyn said. Just then they heard the car in the driveway. Dora began dishing out the spaghetti.

He was wearing tennis shorts and shirt and looked flushed and happy. "Have I got time for a shower?" he asked Dora.

"You and Mark must have had some match," she said to him.

He hesitated, looked at Lyn, and said, "Yes, it was good. Sylvia Maclean was there, too. She seems like a pleasant person." Noticing the food on his plate at the table, he added, "I'd better eat first and then shower."

"I could reheat it," Dora said.

"And ruin great pasta? Never. Lyn and I'll do the dishes. Then we'll get the dog from the vet. You coming with us?"

"Maybe." Dora tugged Lyn's braid playfully as she passed behind her to return a pot to the stove.

Dora didn't suspect anything, Lyn thought, but she did. Dad looked too happy, more cheerful than he had in a long time. She wondered if just talking to Mrs. Maclean—Sylvia—could have excited him that much. Or had there been more to it?

"Did you play tennis with Mrs. Maclean?" Lyn asked.

"What?" Dad asked, as if she'd startled him. Then he said gruffly, "I played with Mark. I told you."

Lyn was satisfied. Dad didn't lie. He believed people should live so that they didn't need to.

"So," Dad said halfway through his spaghetti, "have you thought about inviting the Macleans, Dora?"

"If you want me to, I will."

"Good," Dad said. "How about next weekend? You could make something simple. Everything you cook is excellent."

"Whatever you want."

"The fish stew, then. Come on, Doe," he coaxed. "Don't look so grim. You may like them. Sylvia's easy to talk to."

"You got on a first-name basis with her pretty fast," Dora said.

"Umm." He was too busy eating to see the flash of Dora's eyes, but Lyn saw it.

When Brian, Lyn and Dad entered the examining room, Burlap seemed to recognize them. At least, he tried to stand up, but then he dropped back onto the table, whimpering. Lyn and Brian went to pet him, and Burlap licked Brian's hand.

"You're going to have to keep him very quiet," the vet said. "Put him in a confined area and feed him a soft diet."

"Special food?" Dad asked.

"No, just make the dry dog meal mushy with water or gravy, or use canned food for a while. It'll take a few weeks for that fractured pelvis to heal."

"Do we carry him outside to do his business?" Brian asked.

"No, no. He's able to walk. Moving a little won't harm anything so long as you don't rush him."

Brian insisted on paying the vet's bill. "I want to," he told Dad. "Next time, Lyn can handle it, but I want to this time. Please."

It was painful to watch Burlap limping out to the car, but he went willingly enough. He only balked when he got to it. With all of them pushing and lifting and encouraging him, they finally got him in, but his tail was between his legs, and he whined pitifully.

"As if we're kidnapping him or something," Lyn said.

"Dora should have come. She'd have known how to handle him," Dad said.

Dora had stayed back to comfort one of her boarders, a nervous Sheltie who had refused to eat since her owner had left her the day before.

"Brian's handling Burlap okay," Lyn reported. Brian was sitting on the floor in back with Burlap's head on his lap. The big dog's tail even flapped once in a halfhearted gesture of goodwill.

"I'll come over in the morning to walk him," Brian said.

"If you don't mind, I'll take mornings," Lyn said, "and you walk him after school. I have so many after-school meetings and things."

"Right, okay. And nights. You shouldn't walk him nights. I'll do it."

"Why?" she asked.

"Well, you're a girl."

"It's safe where we live."

"Brian's right," Dad said.

Lyn saw the smile on Dad's face. He liked Brian. Well, so did she, but she wasn't too pleased with the way he seemed to be edging his way into first place in Burlap's affections. The dog's head rested trustingly on Brian's arm. Lyn chided herself for her jealousy. She was getting as possessive as Shelly. But she did wish she could have Burlap sleep beside her bed. It would be so comforting to have the big warm dog close enough to reach out and touch. As soon as he could manage the stairs, she'd move him up from the kitchen, she told herself.

There didn't seem to be a good time that evening to ask Dad about Mrs. Maclean and why he'd come home so buoyed up that afternoon. Anyway, he'd probably accuse her of being nosy, and really she *was* being ridiculous to worry just because he'd held a lady's hands a couple of seconds too long on a tennis court. Relax, Lyn told herself. Dad would never look at another woman now that he was a married man.

FIVE

"Saw your father with his new tennis partner yesterday," Boy Johnson told Lyn as he shoved past her into school. "Wooee! Tell him I admire his taste."

"Tell him yourself," she retorted. His leer left no doubt whom he'd seen. In disgust, Lyn watched him gallop off toward the gym, although she couldn't have said whether her disgust was with him or her father. Learning that Dad had lied yesterday about playing with Mark chilled her. He'd lied, and now she was left wondering what for.

"What's the matter with you?" Jen asked her. "You look sick."

"Nothing. I'm okay."

"You listen to everybody's problems, but you never share your own," Jen complained.

"I *can't* share this one."

In no time Jen had stopped being miffed with her, but Lyn didn't stop churning. The tremors in the ground beneath her feet scared her. She tried to catch her father in the hall to tell him she wanted to talk to him alone as soon as possible, but he wasn't on hall duty, and they had an unwritten rule that she wouldn't walk into his classroom on private business.

Shelly joined Jen and Lyn for lunch. "The cutest boy got moved into my math class and he *smiled* at me," Shelly announced.

Jen raised her eyebrows. "Already?"

"Already what?" Shelly asked.

"You're already over Boy Johnson and onto somebody else."

"Oh, Boy Johnson! That show-off. He looks like a spider with his long skinny legs." Shelly shuddered delicately.

Jen laughed and looked at Lyn, but Lyn was watching her father, who had lunch duty today. His agate-eyed look was settling a rowdy bunch of seventh-grade boys on the other side of the cafeteria. They were meekly handing over the straws they'd been using to blow wads at each other. He'd be looking agate-eyed at her before the day was over, but she didn't care.

That afternoon Lyn finally got to swim practice. It felt good to stretch out in the buoyant water. The movements of her arms and head and legs synchronized, and her strokes smoothed out as she got into a soothing rhythm. The blue pool looked serene through her swim goggles, and since she was the only one there, it was blissfully quiet. Afterward, her body felt boneless and relaxed, even though she tingled with fatigue. Her timing hadn't been off that badly, either.

It occurred to her that Dad might not have been

deliberately deceptive. He could have played with Mark and just hit balls for a few minutes of practice with Mrs. Maclean. His having a friend who was a woman didn't necessarily mean anything was wrong, no matter what stupid kids like Boy Johnson thought. But even so, she didn't like it.

Lyn got home from school to find Burlap in an outside run of the kennel, lying on a hunk of foam mattress Dora had put out for him. He got awkwardly to his feet, wagging his tail as Lyn opened the cage to let him out.

"Hi, handsome. You glad to see me?" she asked him. "Did Brian come by to take care of you?" Knowing Brian, she was sure he had. "Come on, boy. Come in the house with me." She led him by the collar.

Burlap came with her very slowly, favoring his left hind leg. At the back step he hesitated, and Lyn tried to help him into the kitchen. Once there, she rummaged through the refrigerator for some tidbits for him: a meatball, which he took delicately from her fingers with his front teeth, and half a cup of cottage cheese. Politely he lapped up some of the water she offered him, even though he didn't seem thirsty. Then he eased himself down on the vinyl floor in a corner near the back door.

"So, think you'll like it here well enough to stay?" Lyn asked him.

She got out the brush Dora used on Cinder and brushed Burlap's long coarse hair. He rolled over with a groan of pleasure, his front leg flopped out limply so that she could reach his white belly.

46

She was still brushing him when Dora and Dad came in, carrying the weekly food supply. Cinder walked in with them and passed two inches from Burlap's nose before she noticed the big dog. Suddenly she reared back and began yapping in alarm. Burlap watched her calmly, without budging.

"Is she nuts, barking at a dog twice her size?" Lyn asked. Cinder's unexpected aggression surprised her.

"This is her territory," Dora said.

Unimpressed by Cinder's ferocity, Burlap rested his long nose on his paws. Cinder took a step closer, then backed up and barked again before she could get a good sniff of him. Burlap blinked his eyes mildly at her. Cinder minced around to his rear and sniffed his tail. Burlap flapped the tail in goodwill and Cinder flinched, but she took another sniff before strutting off to Dora as if to say, I showed him. Lyn laughed.

"Certainly appears to be a good-natured animal," Dad said, and went back to the car for more bundles. Lyn followed him.

"Dad, can I talk to you for a minute?"

"Umm?"

She took a deep breath and plunged in. "A boy in school gave me the business today about you and Mrs. Maclean."

"What did he say?"

"That she was pretty and that you were playing tennis with her."

"Since when have you let gossip bother you, Lyn?"

"When it's about you. Besides, you told us you'd been playing with Mark."

He hesitated. "All right, I told a white lie. Dora's so

negative about Sylvia, I didn't want to upset her."

"But why do you want to be friends with Mrs. Maclean? People are going to talk about it, and Dora's bound to be upset if she hears."

"Have I ever interfered with your choice of friends, Lyn?"

"No."

"Well, then?" His eyes held her boldly, as if he had nothing to hide. She had always trusted him. She still did.

"Okay," she said. "I just thought I'd tell you."

He touched her shoulder. "Are you worried about Dora or you?"

She thought about it. Did she care if people made snide remarks about her father? Kids had complained to her that he was a strict teacher and marked too hard, but she hadn't ever let it bother her. She could slough off insinuations about his tennis partner, too—so long as there was no truth in them.

"Dora's funny," Lyn said. "She acts strong some ways, and some ways like she needs protecting. And I guess I *am* worried that—well, you don't act as lovey as you used to."

"That's normal after you've been married awhile."

"Then nothing's wrong, Dad?"

Instead of an answer, he posed a question. "Is Dora that good a mother?"

"She's my mother. I waited a long time to have a mother again."

"I suppose you're at an age when having a woman to relate to is important for a girl," he said thoughtfully. Then he touched her shoulder and his eyes were intense as he said, "But don't forget I'm still your father."

It struck her as funny to hear him sounding jealous. Maybe it was going around like a virus, Shelly and Brian, and she herself, and now Dad.

"What are you smiling about?" he asked her.

"There's no way I could forget you're my father," she said.

"That's good." He kissed her, and they headed back into the house as if something had been resolved between them. It was only later when she thought about it that she realized how vague he'd been. He hadn't really told her anything, except that he had indeed lied.

They were just finishing their dessert when Brian knocked on the back door. Lyn let him in. Immediately, Burlap gave him an energetic, tail-thumping, favorite-person greeting.

"Hey, you're feeling better, fella," Brian said with pleasure. He had brought a food offering, which Burlap accepted with dignity, also a new leash. Brian showed it to Dora for her approval. It was a woven nylon strap and harness.

"Looks like the perfect thing for him," Dora said.

"The guy in the pet shop suggested it," Brian said.

It bothered Lyn that she had nothing special to offer Burlap. She could hardly blame the dog for preferring Brian to her, since Brian was the more generous master.

SIX

The Macleans accepted the dinner invitation for that Saturday evening. Dora said she was glad. "The quicker I get this over with, the better," she said.

At the bus stop Friday, Brian asked how Burlap was doing, and Lyn said he had seemed to walk more easily that morning.

"My mother'd like you to leave him locked up outside somewhere when we come to dinner," Brian said.

"No problem. He and Cinder can hang out in the exercise yard. They get along really well."

"I was telling my mother about Spirit Week," Brian said. "She says you're right. It's kind of stuck-up not to go along with it. . . . Well, I guess I can stand making a fool of myself if everybody else does."

"Good. It'll get you in the swing of things."

Brian nodded. "My father has kilts he inherited from my Scottish grandfather. The only thing is, they'll kid me about wearing a skirt."

50

"So? You can take it, can't you? I was a Polish peasant last year. This year I'm going to borrow a Spanish shawl Dad gave Dora and be a señorita," Lyn said. Eagerly, she offered, "If you need something purple, I have a scarf I could lend you."

"No, I'm okay on purple. My mom gave me a purple T-shirt as a joke last Christmas. She thinks I dress too conservatively."

"It'll be interesting to meet your folks. I haven't really had a chance to talk to them yet."

"Yeah." She heard a downbeat tone in his voice and wondered what it meant. But if he had secrets, so did she. Hers was that she planned to assess Dora's competition Saturday evening, if Dora did indeed have competition.

Saturday afternoon Lyn was peeling potatoes for the famous fish stew when Brian knocked at the door.

"You don't have to walk Burlap today," Lyn said. "He's in the exercise yard. Want to come and talk to me instead? Or are you allergic to kitchens?"

"Not me. I'm good in the kitchen." Brian entered confidently.

Lyn gave him the job of slicing and buttering the loaf of Italian bread.

Dora finished setting the dining room table and came back to cut up her salad. "What made you decide to run a kennel?" Brian asked her.

"I like dogs," Dora said.

"Dora wanted to be a vet, but—"

"But I wasn't smart enough," Dora interrupted Lyn to say before Lyn could explain that Dora's mother had died and Dora had had to work her way through college. Nothing had ever been easy for her.

"Dora, don't put yourself down. You are smart," Lyn said.

"Not in school," Dora said. "Teachers made me nervous."

"But you married one," Brian pointed out.

Dora chuckled and said lightly, "Don't ask me how *that* happened."

Lyn didn't think that was funny. "Dora understands animals and people better than anyone," Lyn said. "She just has an instinct about them."

Dora ducked her head and said, "Lyn likes to like the people she likes."

"I've noticed," Brian said.

"Me?" Lyn was startled by the way they were talking about her as if she weren't there.

"I may understand people pretty well," Dora said, "but Lyn's the one who knows how to deal with them best. She'll be a big success someday."

"You're both crazy," Lyn said, but she was pleased as well as embarrassed by Dora's compliment.

The potatoes were peeled and diced. Dora had fresh dill ready for the salad. Gourmet night, Lyn thought. Dora didn't enjoy entertaining, but she was certainly making an effort to do this dinner well.

"Is your mother a good tennis player, Brian?" Lyn asked to revive the conversation, which had died without either Dora or Brian's seeming to notice.

"I guess so. Mom's an achiever. She does most things well," Brian said.

"Do you play?"

"Not really. I'm better at swimming."

"You are? That's my thing," Lyn said. "You ought to join the team in high school next fall."

"Hey, Lyn, haven't you noticed? I'm not a joiner. I do sports for fun. *You're* on a team, I bet."

"I just joined this year. I'm not that good yet."

"Probably you will be. You and my mother. You're both achievers."

Lyn glanced at Dora, who was listening intently. "So, what's bad about that?" Lyn asked.

Brian considered. Finally he said, "Well, it makes Mom restless. Like now she's talking about going back to school to get her master's. My father—he's satisfied just chugging along doing his tax consultant business and gardening and watching TV. He's happy with things as they are."

Brian's mother sounded more interesting than his father to Lyn, but she didn't say anything about it.

Burlap gave Brian a joyous greeting when Lyn and he went out to see the dog. "I think he loves you," Lyn said wistfully, as Burlap pressed his black nose against Brian's arm.

"The feeling's mutual," Brian answered, and surprised Lyn by leaning over to plant a kiss on Burlap's head.

Mrs. Maclean came in, looking glorious in tailored pants and a pink shirt that contrasted with her white hair and vivid blue eyes. "Bruce said you didn't want me to make anything; so we brought the wine," she told Dora.

Lyn thought that side by side the two women

looked like blossom and branch, on a cherry tree maybe, with Mrs. Maclean being the pink and white flowers and Dora being the branch. Plump, mild-looking Mr. Maclean drifted behind his wife as they moved into the living room. There Mrs. Maclean immediately began exclaiming over each of Dora's curiosities: the bird's nest with the blue eggs on the mantelpiece, the geodes on the floor beside the half-dead plants. The living room was so dark that plants were always dying on Dora. A blown-up photograph of a dog Dora had had as a child hung on the wall beside the best armchair. The rest of the decorations were Dad's contribution: Escher prints and a pair of brass lamps with pleated silk shades.

"Oh, Escher," Mrs. Maclean said. "Isn't he intriguing? I bought two of his prints to hang in Morey's study, but he said they made him nervous. Brian took them for his room."

"He's a cerebral artist," Dad said. "Not for people who like their pictures pretty."

"Shouldn't pictures be pretty?" Lyn asked. "What's the point of hanging something that doesn't make you feel good?"

"My husband's on your side, Lyn. Aren't you, Morey?" Mrs. Maclean said.

He nodded agreeably. "I don't know much about art," he said. "I just know what I like."

Quickly, Mrs. Maclean put in, "Morey's been planting flowers all day. Our whole backyard'll be one big flower garden soon."

Mr. Maclean smiled. "Flowers now, you can't plant too many."

"I like flowers, too," Brian said.

"I suspect we've got a consensus on flowers," Dad said. "Anyone who doesn't like them, raise your hand." No one did, which made them all smile.

"You have such beautiful hair," Mrs. Maclean said to Lyn. "I adore long hair. Wish I could let mine grow."

"Why can't you?" Lyn asked.

"Oh, anyone with long white hair would be taken for a witch. My hair's been short since it turned white in my early twenties."

"You're too pretty to be witchy," Lyn blurted out, without intending to.

"Thank you." Mrs. Maclean sounded as pleased as if she'd won a prize.

Lyn glanced at Dora. She stood holding a plate of puffed cheese tidbits she'd apparently meant to offer around but had forgotten about. Dora looked bleak. Concerned, and feeling guilty for having complimented Mrs. Maclean as if Lyn were on her side instead of Dora's, Lyn followed Dora into the kitchen while Mrs. Maclean chatted on with the men.

"Can I help you, Dora?"

"No, thanks. Everything's done." Dora looked around the kitchen. "Everything I'd planned to make. I should have done something besides the fish stew and the salad."

"Why? One bowl of that stew would fill anybody up. It's an elegant meal, and it's Dad's favorite."

Dora had worn her own hair in a braid tonight. A mistake, Lyn thought. It made her thin face look gaunt. "Do you like them?" Lyn asked.

"Do you?"

"I don't know. I like Brian."

"Brian's real. And the father may be okay." Dora moved to the refrigerator. "Go on back out, Lyn. I'm going to mess around here for a while. I'll call you when I'm ready."

Whatever Dora had messed around with for the half hour before she called them for dinner didn't show up on the table. Lyn suspected Dora had just hidden out in the kitchen as long as she could.

The dinner seemed to go well. Mrs. Maclean pronounced the fish stew "superb." Mr. Maclean said it was the best he'd ever eaten. Lyn and Brian cleared away the dishes.

"Dessert's just ice cream," Dora warned.

"Perfect," Mrs. Maclean said. "We're all too full for anything more, aren't we?"

"It was great soup," Brian told Dora.

Dora looked down. She couldn't hide in her hair tonight.

Lyn felt sorry for her and was relieved when Dad followed her out to the kitchen. Maybe he'd say something comforting, like that he loved her. Although Dad could sometimes be dense about Dora's needs. Well, sometimes he was dense altogether. He returned with a glass of ice water for Mrs. Maclean. Dora remained in the kitchen.

"Would you like to come outside and meet Burlap?" Lyn asked the Macleans.

"Not I, thank you," Mrs. Maclean said. "Dogs absolutely terrify me, but I'm really glad that you're sharing it with Brian, Lyn. He's always wanted one, and I've hated depriving him."

"What happened that made you so afraid?"

"Lyn!" Dad said in rebuke, but Mrs. Maclean held up her hand.

Earlier she'd spoken with a lot of animation and hand gestures. Now her eyes spoke as well as she said, "It's not something I talk about ordinarily, but to you, so that you understand—" She took a deep breath and rushed out her words. "I was seven years old and I went to visit my friend after school. Her enormous dog leaped off the porch, right at my face. If I hadn't turned in time—he got my upper arm. I still have the scars. But even before that I was afraid of dogs. My mother was petrified by them, and she must have transferred her fear to me."

"Aren't there psychologists who get you over fears by—" Lyn began.

"No, no, never!" Mrs. Maclean said with a shudder. "I know all about phobia therapy. They subject you to whatever you're afraid of in increasing doses. I'd die."

Dora had finished most of the dishes by the time Lyn and Brian went in to help her. When they all returned to the living room, Mrs. Maclean said, "We've been talking about your hair, Lyn. Don't you ever wear it loose?"

"There's too much of it to let it just hang. It gets messy."

"Oh, but it must be beautiful. Won't you give us a treat and undo the braid? Please?"

Lyn shook her head. She didn't like being on display, and she'd already played up to Mrs. Maclean once this evening when what she'd meant to be was cool and distant for Dora's sake.

"You're going to bed soon, anyway," Dad said. "Come on, honey."

"It's *her* hair," Brian said.

"She'd look like something out of a storybook with it down," Mrs. Maclean said dreamily.

"Lyn's hair is the family treasure," Dad said. "Come on, Lyn. Show it off for me." He looked at her with a foolish smile, and she didn't know how to refuse him.

Reluctantly, Lyn undid the braid while they sat watching her. The silence made her uncomfortable. Halfway through, she dashed upstairs to brush out some of the too regular waviness that braiding always left. Her face was flushed and unhappy in the mirror. She told herself she was being ridiculous, but she didn't feel any less miserable when she finally marched herself back downstairs, where they were waiting for the big show.

Brian took one quick look and turned away, as if he was as embarrassed as she was. Mrs. Maclean went on and on about how gorgeous the hair was.

"Rapunzel had nothing on you, Lyn. May I touch it?" Without waiting for permission, she lifted the heavy mass of hair from Lyn's shoulders and held it out while she exclaimed over it. Dad had a funny grin on his face. Dora glowered in the farthest chair. Only Mr. Maclean looked normal.

"Beautiful," Mrs. Maclean said, and looked at

Lyn's father, who looked back at her as if she were complimenting him. All of a sudden Lyn was furious. She swept her hair out of Mrs. Maclean's fingers and ran upstairs to her own room, where she stood shuddering.

A while later Dora came to tell her that the Macleans had left, and it was okay to come down.

"I don't know what got into me," Lyn said.

"Nothing's wrong with you. It's that woman," Dora said.

"But it was Dad who—"

"Sometimes your father can be pretty much of a fool. It's your hair, Lyn. You do with it what you want."

Dora's visit restored Lyn enough so that later when she was in bed and her father poked his head in at the door to ask apologetically if she was all right, she said, "I'm fine."

"I didn't mean to embarrass you," he said. "I was just showing off my beautiful daughter."

"But I'm not beautiful. I've just got a lot of hair."

"Glorious hair."

But I'm not beautiful, she thought with a pang of regret. It was only in the morning when she woke up that she consoled herself with the idea that it was probably much easier not to be. As to Dora and Mrs. Maclean, inviting the enemy into her home hadn't improved anything for Dora as far as Lyn could see. And Lyn still wasn't sure how attracted Dad was to Brian's mother.

SEVEN

It had rained during the night. Lyn looked out the window at the slick, wet leaves spangled by sunlight and recalled her behavior of the night before with dismay. Getting emotional over nothing wasn't her style. In the light of day she couldn't imagine what had gotten into her. She did her braid up quickly and ran downstairs.

Dad was already immersed in the Sunday *Times*.

"This afternoon could you drive me over to Shelly's, Dad?" she asked. "Her sister's visiting, and I haven't seen Chris since the wedding. She'll probably give me a ride back."

"Is that the sister who quit high school?"

"Shelly only has one sister."

He raised his eyebrow. "Tell me, just what attracts you to that family?"

"Why? Don't you like Shelly?"

"Oh, she's likable. But you don't seem to have a lot in common with her."

"You mean because she's not a student and she's a

little flaky? But she's also lovable, and I can be silly with her. I like being silly once in a while."

He gave her a sympathetic look. "Me, too."

"You, Dad?"

"Playful may be the more apt word in my case."

"Dora's not a playful person," Lyn said tentatively.

"No, she certainly isn't."

He promised to drive her to Shelly's. Lyn kissed him for thanks and went to the kitchen for breakfast. Sundays were busy for Dora, with people picking up and delivering their dogs. Through the back window Lyn could see her being pulled by an exuberant setter toward its owners. Bagels were their usual Sunday morning fare. Lyn toasted one for herself and was spreading it with cream cheese when Dad appeared in the doorway, holding a section of the *Times*. He never went anywhere on Sundays without a piece of the *Times*. It would be spread through the house by the end of the day.

"What would you say to a camping trip Memorial Day weekend?" Dad asked.

"You, Dora and me?"

"Just you and me. It's been a long time since we went anywhere alone. We used to enjoy spending time together, remember? Or have you grown up too much for that?"

His wistfulness touched her. "I'll never be that grown up, Dad," she assured him. "I'd love to go camping with you."

"We could go to Indian Lake."

"Sure, but first let's find out if Dora minds being left at home," Lyn said.

"She won't mind. Memorial Day weekend she'll be busy with her dogs."

Burlap ducked his head and made a sound high in his nose to greet Lyn when she came out to walk him. It wasn't the wild enthusiasm he showed Brian, but it was recognition, at least. "I love you, anyway," she told him as she petted him and put on the harness Brian had bought. "You're my favorite dog, even if I'm only your second favorite person." He gave her a quick lick on the chin, and they set off down the road together.

"We'll stop when you're tired," she promised him. It tickled her that when she spoke to Burlap, he glanced back in response. "You know, you're a smart pooch," she said, but that he didn't bother to acknowledge.

The morning was so fresh and shiny, it made Lyn feel good. A kitten scampered out from under a porch of a farmhouse. Lyn tightened up on the leash when she saw it prancing boldly toward Burlap, but she needn't have worried. The big dog stopped and regarded the kitten with calm curiosity. The kitten meowed expectantly as the enormous face inclined toward it. Burlap sat down on his haunches. Lyn was beginning to think she might have another stray on her hands when the mother cat appeared around the house and yowled at the kitten. Instantly it scampered back to its mother, tail high. Lyn had to laugh at the bemused expression on Burlap's face.

"What a sweetie pie you are," she said. He looked at her and thumped his tail twice on the road. She'd never before responded this strongly to a dog. In fact, some of Dora's boarders had made Lyn think she preferred cats. Burlap was special.

"Maybe you like Brian better than me just because he's male," Lyn said. Dora had said some animals showed a sex preference in humans, usually the sex of their first master. "I hope that's it," Lyn told him, "because I'm just as nice as Brian, really." Burlap stood up and looked at her hopefully, as if he were asking when they were going to continue their walk. "Okay," Lyn said. "Let's go."

Dad drove her over to Shelly's after lunch. He was dressed in the new tattersall shirt Lyn and Dora had given him for his birthday. "Where are you off to, all dressed up?" Lyn asked.

"Thought I might take in that print exhibit at the museum."

"Dora didn't want to go?"

"No, she's busy. And should you hear that I was seen at the museum with Sylvia Maclean, don't be surprised. She may be there."

"Oh?" Lyn said.

He gave her a settling glance. "Next fall Sylvia's going to school in Boston to get her master's in social work. So there's nothing to worry about. Okay?"

Lyn was relieved to hear that Mrs. Maclean was leaving, but next fall was a long time off. And what about Brian? "Are all the Macleans going to Boston?"

"Not as far as I know."

"You mean, they're splitting up?" she asked in alarm.

"Lyn, I don't know," Dad said. "And please, the business about Boston is private. Don't say anything to anyone, not even to Brian."

"I don't understand. They seemed okay together last night."

"Sometimes it takes an X ray to see the fractures," Dad muttered.

She asked him what he meant by that, but they'd arrived. "Enjoy your friends," he said. "You wanted to be silly. Stop worrying and go to it." He kissed her forehead and said cheerily, "See you later."

She slid out of the car and rang Shelly's doorbell. No one answered for a while. Lyn could hear loud music. The music was always loud when Shelly's sister was around. The neighbors had to be deaf not to complain. Finally Lyn tried the door and, finding it unlocked, walked in.

Shelly's sister, Chris, had on a string bikini. Dangling red fringes on the bra and bottom swung wildly as she gyrated in time to the blaring tape. The singer sounded passionate but incomprehensible.

Shelly was standing on the couch wearing a furry tiger suit cut up to the waist on the sides. On her head were tiger ears. Her face was red from laughter. "Come on in. Chris and me are fooling around." She giggled. "These are Mama's old costumes."

Shelly's mother worked in a department store now, but at one time she'd been a dancer. Lyn had never seen the costumes before. Fanciful outfits were spilling from an open suitcase.

"Wow!" Lyn said. "You could put on quite a show with all that."

"Put something on and dance with us," Shelly shrieked. She crouched and pounced onto her sister, who shoved her off and continued dancing.

Chris still hadn't said hello. She seemed to be off in her own world. Lyn had been invited to her wedding last year when Chris had been seventeen, but she really didn't know the older girl well.

Looking over the skimpy, body-revealing costumes, Lyn guessed that Shelly's mother must have been some kind of exotic dancer. The least sexy garment was a feather-trimmed pink satin sheath. Lyn carried it off to Shelly's bedroom, shucked off her pants and blouse, and squeezed into the pink satin. It looked ridiculous with her braid and no makeup; so she borrowed some of the cosmetics strewn on Shelly's dresser to make her face match the costume better. Back in the living room she began shaking and swaying to the music, but carefully, lest she split a seam.

"Lyn, you look fabulous," Shelly yelled. Still in her tiger role, she left her sister to stalk Lyn. A few minutes later, just as Lyn and Shelly were running out of improvisations on their chase and escape routine, Chris threw herself on the couch, burying her face in a velvet cushion.

Lyn froze. "What's wrong with Chris?"

Shelly put her finger on her lips. Still moving to the music, she whispered in Lyn's ear, "Her husband walked out on her, and she lost her job at the hamburger stand."

"But—Chris, are you all right?" Lyn asked. She sat down on the couch next to the half-naked figure, prepared to offer comfort.

Shelly tugged at her arm. "Leave her alone, Lyn. She'll be all right after she tells Mama."

They left the music on and went into the kitchen for some soda. Lyn said someone ought to talk Chris into finishing high school and going to community college. That had been Chris's original plan. But Shelly said, "She can't now. She's pregnant."

"Oh, what a mess!" Lyn said.

"Why?" Shelly asked. "She'll have the baby, and we'll all take care of it. It'll be fun. I never liked Chris's husband, anyway. He was a drag."

Lyn jumped when Shelly's mother suddenly appeared in the hallway and demanded to know what was going on. "What are you girls doing with my costumes? I told you never to touch them. What if I decide to go back on the stage?" Her aging face was grief stricken. "And Lyn, you of all people. I always thought you were such a nice girl."

"She didn't know we weren't allowed," Shelly said. "I didn't tell her you wouldn't let us touch them." Shelly began to cry.

"What's wrong with Chris?" her mother asked, noticing her older daughter still lying corpse like on the living room couch.

Chris sat up and begged, "Mama, don't yell at us. I'm so unhappy."

The mother and her daughters collected in a tight knot on the couch while Chris confessed her problems.

"Well, well, well, now what are we going to do?" Shelly's mother kept saying.

"Chris can move back into my room, and we can put the baby's crib in yours," Shelly said.

"No, you won't," Shelly's mother said sharply. But then, to Lyn's amazement she added, "We'll put the crib in the dinette. I need my rest if I'm going to be the only wage earner in this family."

Quietly Lyn got out of the feathered sheath and washed the makeup off her face. When she was dressed and clean, she presented herself in the living room again and took Shelly aside to say, "I'm leaving, Shell. You guys have a lot to talk over. Tell your mother I'm sorry about the costume."

"Oh, Lyn, I wanted you to have a fun afternoon," Shelly said.

"Never mind. I did. Tell Chris I wish her luck. I'll see you in school tomorrow." She gave Shelly a reassuring smile.

No one thought about how she was going to get home. They were too involved with their own difficulties, but Lyn didn't mind walking. She had a lot to think about, and it was a lovely afternoon. If she took the shortcut along the railroad tracks, she figured it shouldn't take her more than an hour or so.

Funny how things were, Lyn thought. She wouldn't trade her family for Shelly's, and yet under that X ray her father had mentioned, whose family would show fracture signs? She thought of him at an art exhibit with talkative, animated Mrs. Maclean, while Dora went quietly about her chores at home in her doggy-smelling jeans and baggy cotton shirts. It was a depressing contrast and Lyn wished Burlap were with her. She could have used the comfort of his sturdy presence.

Dora was sitting on the back step with her arms wrapped around Cinder, who was asleep on her lap, when Lyn arrived. "Brian's walking Burlap," Dora said.

"And Dad?"

"I'm waiting for him."

Dora looked so tense that Lyn started to ask what was wrong, but just then Dad's car pulled into the driveway. He got out whistling.

"How was the show?" Lyn asked him.

"Interesting. You should have come, Dora."

"Sylvia Maclean called after you left," Dora said. "She asked if you wanted a ride. . . . You didn't tell me she was going, too."

"What difference would that have made?" Dad asked coolly.

Dora hesitated. "None," she said, and dropped her eyes. "None at all," she murmured. She stroked Cinder with her small, callused hands. "What do you feel like having for dinner tonight?"

"I'll make it," he said. "You take it easy, Dora. You look tired." He went inside.

"Dora?" Lyn said, but her stepmother shook her head. "Dora, you can't just sit back. You have to *do* something."

"What? What do you expect me to do?"

"Make him promise not to see her alone."

"I can't make him do anything. If he wants to see her, he will," Dora said.

Lyn couldn't believe that. Something could always be done, and if it didn't work, something else could be tried. Doing nothing, that was giving up. "You can't give up," Lyn said.

Dora didn't seem to be listening. Lyn touched her shoulder to get her attention.

"Don't," Dora said, and moved away.

EIGHT

May was full of its usual chirping baby birds and soft
new grass, but this year Lyn didn't thrill to its promise. She watched Dora hole up inside herself and saw
her father drifting away and couldn't reach either of
them. Burlap was the only family member who
seemed to be thriving. He still showed more enthusiasm for Brian than for her, but Lyn refused to let it
bother her. She worked out her anxiety about her
family by swimming laps in the high school pool and,
lo and behold, helped her team win second place at
their meet, which was far better than they'd expected. Briefly, her teammates made her feel like a hero.

Brian came over Saturday afternoon after the
swim meet to walk Burlap. "So how did it go?" he
asked her once the first wild flurry of Burlap's greeting had subsided.

"Good. I beat my best time and we came in
second."

"Congratulations!" He sounded genuinely
pleased.

In the past few weeks their friendship had deepened enough so that now Lyn could risk urging him, "You know, if you went out for the team next fall, it'd look good on your high school record when the college admissions people see it. You need to go out for something, Brian."

"I don't even know if I'll be here."

"You mean, because of your mother going to school in Boston?" He'd told her that much, but he hadn't been willing to speculate on how it would affect his father and him.

She assumed Brian was still reluctant to talk about it when he shrugged and asked, "You have time to walk with Burlap and me?"

"Sure!" Lyn was pleased. It was the first time Brian had offered to share his time with Burlap with her. "Be back in a while," she called to Dora, who was exercising a Great Dane in the fenced yard.

"Burlap and I usually go up the hill to the field and watch the sunset," Brian said, "but the sun goes down so late now that we won't see it anyway. Want to go somewhere else?"

"The field's fine with me," she said. "I didn't even know you could see sunsets from anywhere around here."

Brian led off up the road past the antiques store. "See, she won't let me take Burlap with us if we move to Boston, or wherever she decides to go to school," he said. Their eyes met briefly, but Lyn saw his misery before he looked away.

"I'm sorry, Brian."

He shrugged. She didn't know what else to say to

comfort him. They kept walking in silence. The country road led them past unused land dotted with white flowering bushes and yellow dandelions and buttercups. Cows grazed in a fenced pasture across from a weary red barn that seemed to have given way at the seams. The ripe odor of manure hung in the air.

"Well"—Lyn offered the only comfort she could find—"you know, if you leave Burlap with me, you could come visit whenever you want."

"Nothing's decided yet, I mean not finally . . . I don't think," Brian said as if he were trying to convince himself. "Dad's still holding out. He never wanted to move here in the first place. He told her that he went through the hassle of moving his business for her once, but he won't do it again. See, with his tax business, it takes him a long time to build up clients who trust him."

"You think he'll give in?" Lyn asked. She could tell by Brian's tone that he sympathized with his father.

"Probably. . . . If I go, you get stuck with all the dog walking."

"Big deal. I don't mind that."

"Of course, I'll continue paying my share of Burlap's upkeep," he assured her earnestly. "I'll just mail you a check every month."

"That's not necessary."

"But I want to. That way, he'll still be my dog a little. . . . Does that sound stupid?"

"No," she said, feeling sorry for him. "I understand. I really do."

"See, I was thinking. Maybe in four years when

I'm finished with high school—well, I could take him then, if I go off to college somewhere that—you know, I don't mean take him from you for good, but—shares."

"That's really long-term planning, Brian."

"Well, but—I don't want to give him up altogether." His light brown eyes had the same gentle, intelligent look Burlap's had as he pleaded with her. "So what do you say?"

She grinned. "I'd be glad to send Burlap off to college with you so long as you ship him back to me for vacations. . . . It sounds like we're divorcing and deciding who gets the kid, doesn't it?"

"Yeah, it does," Brian said.

As if aware he was being discussed, Burlap looked back at them, red tongue dangling jauntily from the corner of his mouth. But his attention was drawn shortly to a spot at the edge of the road that needed a sniff investigation.

"Don't give up yet," Lyn said to cheer Brian. "Your mother could still change her mind."

"Not my mother. Once she decides something, that's it. She made my father leave his family and the friends he'd grown up with in Philadelphia, just because she was itchy. She's a dynamo, like you, and she gets what she wants."

Lyn was stung. "You still think I'm so bossy?"

"No, no. I was complimenting you," he said, and when she looked doubtful, he insisted, "Really, Lyn."

She let it go and asked instead, "Do you want to go to Boston?"

"No way. I like it here."

"Did you tell her that?"

He gave his characteristic shrug. "She asked me what I'd be losing. Like, who my friends here were? Well, you and Burlap were all I could come up with. But it takes me a long time to get into a place. I was just starting to feel at home here."

Indignantly, Lyn said, "I hate the way parents treat us like baggage, like they can just lug us along with them. You should let your mother know you want to stay, Brian." She was angry enough on his behalf to do battle with his mother herself.

Burlap barked after a passing car that had swished by too close to them, then waved the plumy curve of his tail their way and continued up the hill.

"Can *you* get your father to do what you want?" Brian asked.

"Not always, not when it's not what he wants," Lyn admitted, and sighed as she realized she'd just granted the hopelessness of his case.

They had reached the crest of the hill. Brian led the way through a wire fence into a field overgrown with weeds and brambles. He detached Burlap's leash, explaining that he always let him run loose there.

"The sunset view is from the top of those boulders. Want to climb up and sit for a while?"

They climbed onto the scaly boulders. From the top they could see over the hill to the range behind it in the west. Lyn wrapped her arms around her knees and watched Burlap energetically exploring the field.

"I can't believe I've lived here three years and never discovered this spot," she said. "It's fabulous, Brian."

"Burlap likes it."

The only good thing about Brian's leaving was that his mother would go, too. Poor Brian. He was the one losing on all counts. "At least, you'll still be here this summer, won't you?" Lyn asked.

"I don't know. I hope so. I was thinking about lining up yard work."

"Dora might need help if you want to work in the kennel. She'll be busy once vacations start."

"Speaking of vacations," Brian said, "could you possibly take over my dog-walking times Memorial Day weekend? My folks want to go away."

"Sure," Lyn said. "Dad and I are going camping, but Burlap can come, too."

Burlap returned then. He threw himself down at the base of the rocks for a snooze.

"He isn't missing the guy who ditched him anymore," Brian said.

Lyn wondered if Burlap would feel deserted again if Brian left. "Don't worry," Lyn told Brian, "Burlap won't forget you so fast, and anyway, you haven't left yet. Don't give up so easily."

Brian snorted. "*You* never give up. I know."

She considered. "If I think I'm right, I don't. Accepting things doesn't make the world a better place, you know. . . . I admire people who fight for what matters to them."

Brian nodded. "Yeah, like my mother. You know,

what I've said about her doesn't mean I don't like her. She's fun, and she's always interested in what I'm reading and thinking, and she and I get into some pretty hot discussions. Dad and I don't talk much, but he does things with me, like Scouts, and we used to build models together. They're both good people."

"It's nice having two parents," Lyn said, thinking of Dora and Dad. "I wish I came from a really big family with lots of brothers and sisters and aunts and uncles and grandparents. I like family."

"Not *that* much family," Brian said in mock horror. "Just parents is enough for me, thanks."

They had been there long enough to see the sunset, after all. The clouds were lavender against a pale green sky, and a pink wash spread up from the western horizon like a blush. Above them the sky had thinned out to pearly evening as they climbed from the boulders and started home.

Before they parted at Brian's driveway, Lyn thought to ask, "So where are you going Memorial Day weekend?"

"I don't know. They haven't decided yet. My mother mentioned camping, but my father's got allergies."

"Anyway, don't worry about Burlap," Lyn said, and left Brian hastily. She'd promised to make the salad for Dora, and if she didn't hurry Dora would have it done.

In the kitchen, Burlap noisily lapped water from his bowl, which was next to Cinder's. The two dogs had become such good friends that they frequently curled up together with Cinder's paw crooked possessively across one of Burlap's legs.

Dora's hair looked greasy and uncombed. She seemed to be paying less and less attention to her personal appearance lately, Lyn thought. And where was Dad? It used to be that he came home late a couple of days a week. Now it was every day.

To get Dora's mind off where her husband might be, Lyn asked cheerily, "What's doing in the kennel, Dora?"

"Not much. I may start offering grooming."

"I thought you didn't like grooming."

"I'm not wild about it, but the kennel has to bring in more profit."

"Why? You never worried about making money before."

"I'm worried now," Dora said grimly, and went on breading veal patties.

"Dora, are things getting worse between you and Dad?" Lyn blurted out.

"What makes you ask that?"

"Because you're not acting very happy lately."

"I haven't changed," Dora said. "Your father's the one. Ask him what's wrong." She slapped the frying pan down on the stove and Lyn flinched.

Ask Dad, Lyn thought. All right, she would. They'd be alone together for three days of camping. That should be time enough to make him understand that what happened in his life happened in hers, too. So long as she lived with him, she should have some say in the decisions. At the very least, he ought to tell her what was happening. It was scarier to have trouble lurking in the bushes than to face what she could see.

"What's the matter with you?" Jen asked her as they sat side by side in the library the Monday before Memorial Day weekend. "You're going to be the only freshman in high school with frown lines."

"Jen, remember in fifth grade you thought your parents were going to get divorced because they fought so much?"

"They're still fighting except when they're not talking to each other."

"But it doesn't upset you anymore?"

"No. I decided I can't stop them from ending up divorced. I used to get sick to my stomach about it and throw up, and Mother thought I was bulimic or something and took me to the doctor. Now I just shut the door of my room and read."

"That's better?"

"Sure. I've read some terrific books. I even thought I might become a librarian, but ours says she hardly has time to read books these days. It's all paperwork and people problems."

"Maybe you could be a researcher or something like that," Lyn suggested.

"Maybe. Listen, I've got a more immediate problem than my career. Your stupid Spirit Week is coming up. What do you want me to wear for international day?"

Last year Jen had come in regular clothes, claiming she was dressed as an American, which Lyn told her was cheating. With her dark hair tied back, Jen's oval face looked vaguely Indian. Lyn asked, "How about a sari? I know how to drape one if you can get five or six yards of very thin material."

"That sounds painless enough. Okay, I'll bring it to school, and you can drape me in the girls' room that morning."

"Good," Lyn said.

Shelly had been coming to school regularly for weeks and behaving normally for Shelly; so her absence didn't bother Lyn that day. But during an after-school finance committee meeting about the white elephant sale to raise money for year-end activities, Lyn was called to the office for a phone call. She raced downstairs, expecting an emergency at home. The caller was Shelly's mother.

"Lyn, please come help me. Shelly's locked herself in the bathroom. She says she's going to kill herself."

"Why?"

"I don't know. She won't talk to me. She wants you."

Knowing Shelly, Lyn guessed that meant Shelly wanted to be talked out of her despair. "I'll get there as fast as I can," she promised.

She abandoned her committee meeting and hustled over to Shelly's house.

The door opened instantly, and Shelly's mother threw her arms around Lyn and cried, "Thank God, you're here!" Her makeup was tear-streaked and messy, but her dyed hair was carefully combed, and she was still wearing the heels she always wore to work.

"Shelly, you come out of there and stop being stupid," Lyn began forcefully.

"I am stupid," Shelly said. "I'm a jerk and you'll all be better off without me. . . . Where's Mama?"

Lyn looked at Shelly's mother, who gave a half-wave and backed into the living room out of the small hallway.

"She's gone. Do you want her?"

"No. Just you. I did something awful, Lyn. You're going to hate me. . . . You're sure Mama can't hear?"

"Tell me."

"First, promise not to hate me."

"You know I won't. You're my friend, Shell."

Sniffles and sobs came from behind the bathroom door. Then Shelly said, "I went to a boy's house last night? And I stood in the yard under his window?"

"So?"

"So I took my clothes off."

"You're kidding! You did? What'd he do?"

"Nothing. I know he saw me because I saw him looking. Did he say anything?"

"Did who say anything?"

"Brian."

"You took your clothes off in *Brian's* yard?"

Shelly sobbed loudly.

Lyn considered. She couldn't imagine quiet, self-contained Brian spreading gossip. "Shelly, I make you a bet he won't say a word. If he recognized you, which maybe he didn't—it was dark, wasn't it?—

I'll say you were just doing it on a dare. Come out now."

It took another few minutes of coaxing and then Shelly was out, wet and sniffly, but ready to be consoled.

"Do you think I'm crazy, Lyn? Do you think I should see a shrink?"

"I don't know. Why don't you see the school counselor and ask if there's some test you can take to find out?"

"You *really* think I'm crazy?" Now Shelly was insulted.

"Well, what you did sounds a little strange."

Shelly's mother, who'd been hovering just out of sight in the living room, reappeared and put on a dramatic performance of mother love and concern. Lyn began to feel like an extra. But when Shelly's mother drove Lyn home with Shelly along for the ride, all Lyn heard was what a wonderful friend she was, and how they didn't know what they'd do without her.

"Just come to school tomorrow," Lyn said. "I'll deal with Brian." They appreciated her so much and listened to her so attentively. Lyn wished she had half as much influence with her own father as she had with them.

Dora had a customer with a dog in the glassed-in front porch she used as an office. Lyn dialed Brian's number and got him on the phone. "I understand you had something interesting to look at in your backyard last night."

"You mean she told you?"

"That's why she stayed home from school today. Didn't you notice? She's scared of being teased."

"Tell her not to worry. I don't even feel comfortable talking about it to you."

Lyn laughed with relief. "Shelly's really a good kid," she said.

"If you say so," Brian said.

He was nice, Lyn thought, so nice. She was really going to miss him a lot if he moved away, even if he took his mother with him.

NINE

Even though she was looking forward to having her father to herself for a weekend, Lyn began trying to talk Dora into going with them the minute after Dad left for his teachers' meeting that evening.

"You could hire the boy who worked for you last summer when your hand was in a cast, Dora. You said he was good with the dogs."

"I have some thinking to do, and I do it best alone."

"But you're alone every day."

"Thinking takes me lots of time." The sad edge of Dora's smile made Lyn want to cry

"Please, Dora. Come with us. For me."

"But it wouldn't change anything if I went," Dora said, "not between your father and me."

"Think of what fun we have when the three of us vacation together." Lyn was dangerously close to coming right out and saying that it wasn't going to be the three of them for long the way things were going, but she didn't want to hurt Dora. So she continued with the positive approach.

"Remember the last camping trip when Dad couldn't figure out how to set the tent up, and you got it to work right? And you know he'll overcook the hamburgers without you."

"He likes his hamburgers overcooked, and he knows how the tent works now. So do you. He's looking forward to having you to himself, Lyn."

"Oh." Was that why Dora wouldn't come? A warm pleasure curled up in Lyn that her father also missed the special closeness they had had before he married Dora.

Energetically, Lyn set about preparing for the trip. She collected Burlap's blanket, bowls and leash, a new flea and tick collar, a flashlight—Dad was sure not to think of flashlights, nor ponchos in case of rain—their sleeping bags, of course, and rolls of foam to put under them to blunt any stones or tree roots. She packed towels and soap and insect repellent, bathing suits and sweaters for the evenings, matches, lots of matches, and a bag of charcoal, as well as the set of camp cookware they'd never used. She carried a list with her and added things to it as she remembered: first aid kit, cards and books, suntan lotion.

Shelly was happy because, for a change, the boy she liked liked her and she was a couple. "I don't need a shrink now. Love has cured me," Shelly assured Lyn. She asked if Lyn and Brian wanted to double-date to a movie.

"I don't think Brian's ready for dating," Lyn said.

"He and I are friends, but not boyfriend-girlfriend."

"You mean," Shelly said, "he doesn't even kiss you?"

"Well, he almost shook hands with me once," Lyn joked, but Shelly didn't laugh.

It was raining Saturday morning. Dad hated rain, and Lyn immediately began to worry that he'd delay the camping trip, but to her surprise he was at the breakfast table before her, wearing a plaid flannel shirt and his oldest jeans.

"All that gear'll never fit in the car, not with us and a man-sized dog to boot," he grumbled.

"Sure it will. That's what you always say before a vacation."

He grunted, unable to deny that he did always say it and that things did always fit. "Dora made us some cookies," he said.

"Dora's a sweetie pie. Think we can fit the cookies in, Dad?"

"Don't mock me. What I need is praise and encouragement. I must be crazy to be going camping in weather like this."

"You're a sweetie pie, too," Lyn said, "and as to the rain, I promise it'll stop before we get there."

"All right. Eat your breakfast and I'll start packing the car." His grin gave him away. He was as eager to go as she was.

Lyn found Dora hosing down the kennels and kissed her good-bye. "You'll miss us a little, won't you?" Lyn asked.

"Maybe a little," Dora admitted with a smile. "You have fun now."

Lyn hurried back to where Dad was shoving the last of their equipment into the car. She tried to get Burlap in, too, but neither coaxing nor tugging worked.

"Leave him home if that's how he feels," Dad said. "It'll give us more breathing space."

"Please, Dad, help me with him." Winning Burlap's affection was part of Lyn's secret agenda for this camping trip.

"All right, all right." Dad got behind Burlap and shoved. Finally, the dog let himself be pushed into the front seat, where he stood, tail down and trembling.

"You're going to love camping," Lyn told him. "New smells, maybe even a skunk or fox." He didn't seem impressed. The last time Burlap had ridden in a vehicle had been to and from the hospital, she realized, and before that he'd been dumped from a truck by a beloved master. No wonder he was scared. She put her arms around his solid neck and hugged him. "I'd never leave you, never," she assured him.

They took off, and Burlap finally settled down on the seat between them. His head was on a level with theirs as he looked out the front window. Every so often his caramel eyes fixed on Lyn anxiously, and she petted him.

"Next time, instead of camping, we should take a city vacation," Dad said as they turned onto the two-lane highway toward the lake region. "You've never been to Boston, have you?"

The mention of Boston chilled Lyn. "I thought you liked the country," she said quickly.

"I do. It's a good place to read and contemplate your navel, but the cultural offerings are sparse. Do you remember when we lived in New York City and even a walk around the block was an adventure?"

"I remember the roaches at night and all the garbage in the streets."

"That's all?"

"Well, I was only seven or eight then, Dad."

"You'd feel differently now. And Boston isn't New York."

She swallowed hard. "Are you trying to tell me something?"

"No," he said. "I've just been thinking."

"About Mrs. Maclean going to Boston?"

"About Boston," he said. "About changing my life."

Lyn stared out at the pinkish white blossoms of an apple orchard without registering their beauty. If he was thinking about changing his life, he meant to change hers as well, whether he recognized that or not. "And what about Dora?"

"What about her?"

"She wouldn't want to move, would she?" Lyn stiffened to withstand the answer and asked herself why she had to ruin the weekend by finding out what was in the bushes so soon.

"I don't expect Dora would give up her kennel for anything."

"But she hasn't been very happy lately."

"She's not basically a happy person, Lyn."

"Then why did you marry her?" Lyn burst out.

"I thought I was going to make her happy. I imagined I could give her what she needed, but it turns out I have needs, too, and Dora doesn't care to meet them."

"Why? She tries hard. She's always cooking something you like, and she's a good mother. Just because she doesn't care about clothes—"

"Lyn, I'm not going to go into all the ways in which Dora and I fail each other. That's very private stuff."

"Are you telling me that you're going to get a divorce?" Her voice sounded shrill and breathless in her own ears.

"It's one of the options I'm considering."

"And don't *I* get considered?"

He glanced away from the road to look at her. It was a loving look, and his tone was sympathetic as he said, "Sure you do. I know you love Dora and want everything to stay as it is. I know that, Lyn. If I weren't considering you, I'd have made a move by now."

"To Boston?"

"I don't know, honey. I don't know anything for sure. You're going to have to be patient with me. Okay?"

She concentrated on breathing, one careful breath at a time. Boston was where Mrs. Maclean wanted to go. Could he decide to go with her, just like that, when they were both married to other people, as if being married were no big deal? Burlap licked Lyn's cheek. She hugged him and said to her father, "When you got married, you promised to stay together. What good is a promise if you can break it so easily?"

"Not very good," Dad said. "Lyn, I already feel like a failure. You don't have to rub it in."

"You're not a failure," Lyn said. "You were happy with my mother, weren't you?"

"I think so, but we had our quarrels. And she got killed before—I don't know, Lyn."

Lyn held her breath. Her heart was beating so fast. What was he telling her? Was her image of her mother a fairy tale then? They had been a happy family before the car crash that Mother had died in. They had been happy. At least, that was how she remembered it, and she didn't want to remember it any other way. He had no right to ruin that, too.

"Incidentally," Dad said, and stopped to negotiate the turn from the highway onto the county road that skirted the reservoir and led into the pine- and spruce-covered foothills toward Indian Lake. "We might bump into the Macleans this weekend. Sylvia asked me where they could find a good camping spot, and I told her about Indian Lake."

It was the second shock of the morning. Lyn stared at her father's boyish profile as if she'd never seen it before, and said carefully, "I thought it was just going to be the two of us."

"So it will be. It's a big camping area. Even if they're there, it's unlikely we'll meet them, especially if you don't want us to."

She mulled that over. It sounded reasonable. Calm down, she told herself, and stop being so quick to conclude the worst. So the Macleans might be in the campground. Well, if they did meet, she wouldn't mind sharing a campfire with Brian and his father some evening. Sylvia Maclean was the only one Lyn wanted to avoid, wanted Dad to avoid.

They passed a store that specialized in deerskin products. Bait for sale, a sign said. The road wove, steep and narrow, through the dark evergreen woods. "Talk to me," Dad said as the silence took on weight.

"What about?"

"I don't know, honey. Anything that interests you."

She started telling him about Shelly and some of the antics that made Lyn worry about her. "She's such a kook. I wish I knew how to help her."

"It's not your responsibility to help her. You forget you're only a kid yourself."

"And kids can't be responsible? Come on, Dad. Some of us are better at it than you so-called adults."

"Is that a dig at me?" he asked.

"Well, I'm not too thrilled with what you're doing to our life—*our* life, not just yours."

"I told you, I'm not doing anything except thinking."

She sighed. She wished she could argue better. She wished she could make him understand her point of view. No matter how many words she used and how calm she tried to stay, he could always evade her or turn things around somehow. "Anyway," Lyn said, "I hope Shelly gets interested in something besides boys or she's going to end up like her sister."

"Tell you what," he said. "I've got to recommend a

student to be a counselor's aide for the youngest kids in the playgrounds this summer. Do you think Shelly could manage that?"

"She might do well. She loves little kids, and that'd keep her busy. Yes, that's a great idea, Dad. I'll ask her if she's interested. . . . Thanks." She knew that it was for her sake he was willing to help Shelly, and she was grateful.

They drove past old-fashioned motels consisting of individual cabins that looked too small to hold a full-sized bed, and bars with names like "The Blue Bottle Inn." Trailers with propane tanks beside them were decorated with lines of washing and children's toys. The sign for the state park was so small they missed it and had to backtrack when a gas station attendant told them they'd come too far.

The rain stopped just as they drew up to the wood-shingled booth where fees were collected and campsites assigned. Lyn took the sunlight as a good omen. They were going to have fun together—just that would be enough for the weekend.

With the help of a map of the extensive camping areas, they found their campsite on a knoll above the lake.

"We lucked out," Lyn said. "This *has* to be the prettiest spot."

Burlap jumped out of the car and promptly lifted his leg against several bushes to mark his territory, then lolloped down to the water's edge, plunged in and took a swim. They were unloading their gear when he climbed back up and shook cold water all over them.

"Stop that, you canine lawn sprinkler, you!" Dad howled.

Lyn tied Burlap to a tree with a long rope brought for that purpose. He settled down happily to watch them. Lyn had to giggle as her father struggled to get their tent set up. "I was sure I remembered how we did it the last time," Dad said.

"How Dora did it," Lyn reminded him. "Anyway, it's stopped raining and we don't need the tent until tonight."

"It's going up now." He returned determinedly to dealing with poles and nylon sheets and rope and pegs. Lyn laid out their cold lunch on the thick wooden picnic table next to the open-topped iron grill on which he would overcook their hamburgers later.

"Ah-hah," he said with proud relief as the tent finally took the shape of a proper shelter. "Told you I could do it."

They ate their sandwiches hungrily, and Dad suggested they see about renting a canoe.

"Sure," Lyn said. "Or we could try a hiking trail."

"Whatever you prefer."

"Well, what do you want to do?"

"Actually," Dad admitted, "I wouldn't mind a little catnap in the sun before we tackle anything else."

"You catnap and I'll go for a walk with Burlap."

"Don't get lost."

She set off to explore, not thinking about the Macleans or Dora or anything unsettling. She needed time to digest what her father had told her before she decided what, if anything, she could do about it.

She turned off the narrow, paved park road onto a dirt road into the woods and came upon a colony of campsites so cleverly tucked into niches among the tall trees that each had some special feature: a miniature waterfall, or a natural rock garden. Many were set beside a clear, shallow stream. Lyn walked Burlap onto the arched wooden bridge that spanned the stream. She was admiring the colorful mosaic of water-glazed stones below when a familiar car pulled into the nearby campsite. Lyn scrambled to get off the bridge and out of sight. Too late. Burlap barked and pulled so hard to get to the car and Brian that he yanked the leash out of her hand.

Trapped, Lyn stood still, watching Mrs. Maclean and Brian get out of their car. Just Mrs. Maclean and Brian. Lyn blinked, but Mr. Maclean didn't materialize from the backseat. Brian was nearly knocked over as Burlap leaped on him in a tail-wagging frenzy. Mrs. Maclean screeched and jumped back in the car.

Grimly, Lyn went over to reclaim Burlap.

"Hi," Brian said, handing her the leash. "You sure found us quick."

"I wasn't looking for you," Lyn said. "Where's your father?"

"He couldn't come. One of his clients wanted to see him, or so he said. I don't think Dad's keen on camping. He's got a lot of allergies."

"I see," Lyn said tonelessly.

"What's wrong?"

"Nothing. I better take Burlap away so your mother can get out of the car."

"Lyn, hold up a minute," Brian said. *"What's wrong?"*

"They planned this. Or, anyway, I bet your mother did—so they could be together."

Brian just stood there, looking stunned. Lyn didn't care if she'd upset him by accusing his mother of tricking them. She was too angry to care. Pulling Burlap away from Brian with all her strength, she headed back to her own campsite. There she found her father still asleep in a string hammock he'd hung between trees. His mouth was open, and a lock of hair was tickling his forehead. He looked so innocent. Had he known Mrs. Maclean was coming without her husband? If he had planned to meet that woman here, Lyn would never forgive him and never believe him about anything ever again, either.

As soon as Dad woke up, Lyn said, "Guess who I bumped into on my walk."

He stared at her. "The Macleans? Already? That's a coincidence. Where are they?"

"Five minutes' walk from here." She didn't mention that the father hadn't come. "Let's go rent a canoe now, huh?"

"What's the rush? Maybe they need some help setting up camp."

"No. Brian'll handle it. Come on, Dad, let's go."

He hesitated, then shrugged and went to change into his bathing trunks. She stood on the rock, staring out over the dark green water of the island-studded lake. The best she could do now was to stick by her father's side and see to it that he didn't have a chance to spend time alone with Mrs. Maclean.

Burlap panted quietly, his eyes on her. "You better not decide to go visit Brian," she told the dog. "You'll give his mother a heart attack."

"Woof," Burlap said as if in answer, and Lyn hugged him, her furry comforter.

They took their time getting used to balancing in the canoe. Dad had said sensibly that they'd better follow the shoreline in case they tipped over. When they finally got the hang of paddling without zigzagging too much, they'd been at it a couple of hours, and he complained that his knees hurt from kneeling on the cushion in the bottom of the canoe.

"Let's pull up on an island and go for a swim. It's warm enough," Lyn said. She wanted to delay their return as long as possible.

"You go. I'll watch," Dad told her. She thought about getting her braid wet and the difficulty of undoing it and drying it, and decided to skip the swim. They pulled the canoe back up on shore at the landing.

No sooner had they finished than Dad said, "Look who's coming." He sounded much too happy about it.

Mrs. Maclean looked cute in skimpy, gray-knit sweat shorts and matching shirt, with a red headband around her forehead to hold her flashy white hair back. Brian was a step behind her.

"Hi there, having fun?" Mrs. Maclean greeted Dad and Lyn.

"How about a canoe ride?" Dad suggested.

"Love one," she said.

Before Lyn could mention the stiff knees or that Brian might like to go canoeing with his mother, Dad had helped Mrs. Maclean in and shoved off. He soaked his sneakers in the process without even noticing it.

Brian cursed, which was unusual enough for him to make Lyn ask, "Are you thinking the same thing I think?"

"I don't like being tricked," Brian said.

"Do you think she meant to come without your father?"

"She? Your father's just as bad. The way he looks at my mother makes me sick."

Lyn's hackles rose and she would have attacked, but then she realized it was true. Her father had lit up with admiration and excitement when he saw Mrs. Maclean come toward them just now. He'd looked at Mrs. Maclean the way Shelly looked at boys she had a crush on. Her father, her father whom she'd trusted.

TEN

Lyn woke up and tried to figure out where she was. Burlap's head and massive shoulders, outlined by the moonlight shining into the entrance to the tent, set her straight. She had gone to sleep with Burlap lying across the foot of her bag. Now he sat in the doorway. She glanced at her father's sleeping bag. It was empty.

"Dad?" she called softly, as if he might be hidden somewhere in the tight confines of the tent. She crawled to the screened opening and squeezed out past Burlap. The campsite held the shadowy statuary of picnic table and car and trees, but no father. He'd probably gone to the public bathrooms, which were in a clean, well-lighted building a short walk down the road. It was the only place he could go in the middle of the night unless— No, she chided herself. Don't be nasty. They hadn't even had dinner with the Macleans. So far, the only time Dad and Mrs. Maclean had been together was in the canoe.

Unable to fall back to sleep, Lyn walked to the

edge of the campsite near the lake. There she sat down on a rock and wrapped her arms around her knees against the chilly air. Burlap padded after her and nudged her arm with his head. His warm body felt good against her side. She held him close while she waited for her father.

An eerie icing of moonlight covered the lake below a dark blue sky speckled with star crystals. For a while, Lyn sat listening to the peeping of frogs, rustlings in the bushes, leaves whispering. Then she began stewing about where her father was. He could easily have gotten lost on his way back from the bathroom and be bumbling around in the dark through strangers' campsites. She considered forming a rescue party with Burlap, but decided if she missed Dad in the dark, he might panic on returning to the tent to find her gone.

Yawning, Lyn leaned her head against Burlap to doze. She woke chilled and damp and still alone. She'd left her watch home because it wasn't waterproof, but surely hours had passed. Where was Dad? She began imagining wild things, that a bear had chased him up a tree or he'd fallen into the lake. Or—or he could be meeting Mrs. Maclean somewhere. Hastily, Lyn squelched that notion.

She returned to the tent to look for the flashlight but couldn't find it. Burlap whimpered for her. "Let's go look for him, anyway, Burp," she said, because suddenly she couldn't stand another minute of waiting. She grabbed her jacket out of her pack and let Burlap lead her through the dark alley of bushes to the road. There a flashlight beam found her.

"Lyn, what are you doing up?" Dad asked.

"Looking for you. Where were you?"

"Call of nature," he said.

"You've been gone for hours."

"It felt like hours to me, too. I got lost and terrified some poor lady by trying to crawl into her tent. It's bizarre how different things look at night."

It sounded reasonable. Lyn didn't mention Mrs. Maclean. He'd be hurt by her suspicions. Once he had told her that his Methodist grandmother sat in a rocking chair inside his head, watching him. "I wouldn't dare misbehave with Grandma Kellem watching." Lyn hoped Grandma Kellem remained on guard duty.

In the morning she took Burlap for a walk and found Brian fishing from the bank of the lake. Brian returned Burlap's lavish greeting with one hand while he hung onto his pole with the other.

"Catch anything?"

"Not yet," Brian said.

"Want to try fishing from our canoe? Dad rented it for the weekend."

Brian looked puzzled. "Didn't your dad tell you? The plan is for us all to go canoeing after breakfast." He spoke to Burlap, "All except you, fella. You get to mind Lyn's tent. Okay?"

Burlap barked as if in agreement.

"When was that decided?" Lyn asked.

"Beats me. Yesterday, maybe?"

"Brian, did your mother leave your tent last night?"

He stared at her. "Why are you asking?"

"Just answer me."

"I can't. I was asleep and when I sleep, nothing wakes me up. . . . What happened? Did your father take off during the night?"

She hesitated, then said lamely, "I guess he just went to the bathroom and got lost. I got nervous because he was gone so long, but he probably did just get lost."

"We can't be their chaperones," Brian said quietly. "Anytime they want, they can drive somewhere and meet each other without us knowing."

"My father wouldn't lie to me."

"That's nice, but I don't know about my mother," Brian said. "She's covered her tracks plenty of times with what she calls little white lies. She says they're to keep my father from worrying." Some of the heat went out of his voice and he added, "But basically, she's straight." His bobbin dipped, and he pulled in a ridiculously small sunny.

"Anyway, it's a beautiful day," Lyn said, making the best of things as Brian detached the sunny and threw it back, "and we might as well enjoy it. Maybe we can tie the canoes up to some island and go for a swim."

They met at the landing an hour later. Mrs. Maclean had rented a second canoe. Dad and Lyn drew theirs up next to it. "Who's the canoeing expert in the Maclean family?" Dad asked.

"Brian," Mrs. Maclean said. "He's gone on canoe trips with the Boy Scouts. He's even portaged." She was wearing the same skimpy gray shorts she'd worn yesterday. Today her legs had goose bumps. It would be warm later, but at midmorning it was still damp and chilly under the pines.

"Well, Brian," Dad said, "if you trust me with your mother, I'll trust you with my daughter."

Brian looked at Lyn. "Okay with you?"

"We'll keep the canoes close together, won't we?" she asked the adults.

"I suspect it's me she doesn't trust, Brian," Dad said. "The first time I took her out in a canoe, I got a little close to the lip of a dam, and she's never forgotten it."

"Oh, come on, you guys," Mrs. Maclean said. "This'll be fun. Let's go."

"My mother's the risk taker in our family," Brian said. "Dad and I, we think of things like insect spray and flashlights and emergency flashers."

Mrs. Maclean tossed her head. "Oh, you!" she said. "So I forgot a few things. So what? If you think I'm going to share a canoe with you so you can put your poor old mother down all morning, forget it." She promptly climbed into the first canoe. "You pushing us off, or shall I?" she asked Lyn's father.

He followed after her, grinning. "I'll do it," he said. Again he got his sneakers wet.

"You tease her a lot," Lyn said to Brian when the parents were out of earshot.

"Well, I laid that stuff out, and she forgot it. And on the way up here I found out that she doesn't even know where the emergency flasher is in her own car. . . . You want bow or stern, Lyn?"

"You can steer us. I'll take bow," she said.

Brian handled the canoe well, better than her father, whose canoe was making somewhat erratic progress up the lake ahead of them. Mrs. Maclean's infectious laugh carried back to them. Lyn tried to remember what Dora's laugh sounded like and couldn't. Dora wasn't much of a laugher, but Lyn wished she'd come, all the same.

The paddle dipped neatly into the thick green water, pushed and came up dripping, cut in and back against the water resistance. Again it dipped, and then again. The easy rhythm was soothing in the silence of midmorning. They passed a boat with two crumpled-looking fishermen and nodded without saying anything. Their canoe quickly caught up with the lead one.

"We going to stop somewhere for lunch?" Brian yelled a while later.

"What lunch?" Lyn asked.

"We brought some," Mrs. Maclean called back. "Wonderful fat chicken salad sandwiches. Yum. All this fresh air and exercise's made me hungry already."

"You pick the island, Brian," Lyn's father said.

Brian surveyed the lake ahead of them and pointed. "The one with the pine tree and the smooth rock down to the water's edge. Let's see if we can pull up there."

"We'll race you," Mrs. Maclean challenged.

"We will not," her captain said. "They're younger than we are."

"But we're stronger. Come on, lazybones, pull."

Dad's chagrin tickled Lyn. Except for tennis, he was happier lying in a hammock, reading, than doing anything physical. Still, he seemed to be pulling his hardest for Mrs. Maclean. In fact, their canoe shot ahead at first, and Mrs. Maclean let loose with an Indian war whoop.

"Okay," Brian said. "Let's get 'em."

Lyn felt the canoe scoot forward with the increased power of his thrust, and she matched his strokes, caught up in the competition. Halfway to the island, they slid past their parents' boat and were there standing in the shallows on the rock to land it when it arrived.

"To the winners go the spoils," Mrs. Maclean said good-naturedly as she handed over the plastic picnic bag to Lyn. The four of them settled down to picnic on the warm hide of the lichen-mottled rock.

"What a day!" Mrs. Maclean said. "It feels more like the end of June than the end of May."

"Warm enough to swim after lunch," Brian said.

"Umm, I'll have to think about that," his mother informed him. "Nice as it looks, I bet that water feels like ice cubes."

"These are delicious," Lyn said of the chicken salad sandwiches.

"Aren't they? Brian made the chicken salad yesterday and packed it in ice. He's a good cook."

"A man of many parts," Dad said. "What other talents do you have, Brian, besides cooking and canoeing?"

"Not much," Brian said.

"He swims well," his mother said. "And he's a good student. In his quiet way, he does most things well."

"Not as well as Lyn," Brian said.

The compliment took Lyn by surprise, and she blinked at him.

"Well, it's true," Brian said. He turned to her father. "Wouldn't you rate her outstanding?"

"I'm very proud of my daughter," Dad admitted.

"Well, aren't we the congratulatory bunch!" Mrs. Maclean teased.

They busied themselves eating their sandwiches and drinking cans of juice. Brian finished first and went to explore their living-room-sized island. "Should have brought my fishing rod," he said when he came back. "There's a hole in the rocks on the other side that's bound to have fish."

His mother yawned and said, "You could go back and get the rod."

"Too much trouble."

They lay about sleepily in the sun for a while after lunch, talking. Dad told a story about a school camping trip he'd chaperoned when a boy swore a bear had looked into his tent, and everybody stayed up all night waiting for its return. "Nobody slept except on the bus going home," Dad said.

That reminded Mrs. Maclean about her camping experience with a group of juvenile offenders she'd worked with one summer. She had been a social worker in Philadelphia. "Just making a fire or pitching their own tent was enough to start them feeling a little good about themselves," she said.

Dad winked at Lyn. She kept quiet about his past difficulties with tents and fires, so as not to embarrass him.

A while later Lyn announced it was time for a swim. She stripped down to her swimsuit and did a shallow dive off the island near where they'd beached the canoes. The water was an icy shock. She swam vigorously toward the middle of the lake to warm herself up. They were all still standing there watching her when she returned.

"How is it?" Dad asked.

"Nice!"

"Youth may say nice," Mrs. Maclean said, "but my big toe says ouch." She had her sandals off and her toe delicately tested the water.

"Come on, Brian," Lyn said. "You're supposed to be a swimmer."

He grunted, then complained, "We don't even have towels to dry off with."

"The sun will dry you off," his mother said.

Brian shucked his jeans and T-shirt. He was wearing trunks.

"Want a push?" Dad asked.

"No, thanks," Brian said. He took a running start and dove in, coming up yards from shore behind Lyn. "Yeow!" he yelled. "You'd have to be a polar bear to call this nice." Then he began swimming. Lyn admired his economical crawl for a few seconds before following him. Glancing back, she saw her father and Mrs. Maclean draw close to each other in conversation. Well, they wouldn't be there alone for long.

Fifteen minutes later, Lyn and Brian had circled the island and climbed out to warm themselves on the stone. "That was fun," Lyn said.

"Yeah," Brian agreed. "A lot of outdoor stuff is hard to make yourself do, like getting into cold water or hiking up a mountain, but it's always worth it."

"Spoken like a good Boy Scout," Dad said.

Unself-consciously, Lyn began undoing her braid to dry her hair in the sun. No one commented, and she felt as comfortable as if they were all family.

"Shall we head back?" Dad asked midway through the afternoon. "Or do you want to canoe further down the lake?"

"I'm for heading back," Mrs. Maclean said. Thinking of Burlap alone at their campsite, Lyn agreed.

"Need help braiding your hair?" Mrs. Maclean asked her.

"No, thank you. I can manage."

"Time was when doing Lyn's hair was my job," Dad said wistfully. "I felt rejected when she didn't need my help anymore."

"Did you really? I didn't know that," Lyn said.

Paddling back, Brian kept well behind their parents' canoe. It struck Lyn that Sylvia Maclean and Dad matched better than Dora and he did, in personality and looks and probably in interests as well. But it was Dora he had married, and Mrs. Maclean was married, too. And they were parents. They couldn't fall in love with each other now. It would be wrong.

"You're paddling crooked," Brian said. "Relax."

She eased up on her stroke. "It's funny with parents," she said. "When you're little, all you care about is winning their approval, and you accept however they are, but then you get older and look at them critically and see their faults."

"Right," Brian said.

"But you're judging them on the principles they taught you, really."

"Not always," Brian said. "We learn from society, too, and what we read and from teachers and other kids."

"Umm," Lyn murmured neutrally. But she knew who had taught her her values.

The four of them made dinner together at the Maclean campsite and then played a Boggle game that Mrs. Maclean had brought along. She even wanted them to sing a camp song when the embers in the fireplace were an incandescent red in the darkness, but Dad and Brian refused. Burlap was the only one who hadn't enjoyed the evening. He'd had to stay tied up at the other campsite.

"Burlap's a wonderful dog," Lyn had said when she was trying to coax Mrs. Maclean into letting him join them.

"I know he is. I know it here." Mrs. Maclean pointed to her head. "But, Lyn, I can't tell you how panicky I get when he's loose and I'm anywhere near him. I'd like to control it, but really I can't."

"I understand," Lyn said, although she wasn't sure she did.

"I wish I *could* do something about it," Mrs.

Maclean said regretfully. "For Brian's sake. He's crazy about that dog."

"I know. Burlap loves him a lot, too," Lyn said.

Mrs. Maclean looked at her earnestly. "My son's a very special boy," she said. "But he doesn't make friends easily. I'm glad you and he have become friends."

"Thank you." Lyn was pleased. Then she felt guilty about being pleased. Brian's mother was likable, but Lyn had to resist liking her for Dora's sake as well as her own.

To make it up to Burlap for his banishment, Lyn took him for a very long walk before bedtime. Both of them were physically tired when they got back. That night Lyn slept soundly.

ELEVEN

Monday morning, Memorial Day, came up cool and foggy. "Looks like a good day to give up on camping and go home early," Dad said on his return from the bathroom.

Lyn had checked out the weather, too. "Well," she said, "the fog's bound to lift, and meanwhile we could hike up one of the trails. I bet we'd be in the clear if we climbed up a way."

"Whatever you like, honey," Dad said. "I'll go tell Sylvia and Brian our game plan while you finish your cereal."

Suddenly, his assumption that they had to check in with the Macleans enraged Lyn, and she burst out with, "What happened to all the time we were supposed to spend alone together?"

He looked startled. "All right, we'll hike by ourselves if that's what you want."

They cleaned up after breakfast and were setting off with a map of the park and Burlap when Brian and Mrs. Maclean showed up. Mrs. Maclean kept her distance from Burlap, who barked and wriggled and even raised his upper lip in a smile for Brian.

"What are you guys up to on this misty morning?" she called to them.

Dad glanced at Lyn, but she waited until he answered. "We're going to see if we can hike up out of the fog."

"What a good idea!" Mrs. Maclean said. "Mind if we join you?"

Now both Dad and Brian eyed Lyn. She couldn't bring herself to be rude. The best she could do was try to discourage Mrs. Maclean by warning her, "Burlap's coming with us."

"On a leash, I hope," Mrs. Maclean said cheerfully. "You and Brian can lead the way with him, and I'll keep a safe distance back."

Brian's face was unreadable. Lyn turned away and pretended to adjust the canteen, which was slipping off her shoulder. Dad cleared his throat.

The five of them set off up the road in a mist so thick they seemed to be walking through a cloud. The nearest hiking trail began at a fence post and was marked with yellow plastic tags on trees. It was supposed to be a mile-and-a-tenth hike up to a waterfall. "Up" was accurate. When they'd climbed a short way from the road, they were out of breath, but out of the mist, too. Ahead of Lyn, Brian was being hauled up the mountain by Burlap on a short leash. Lyn's worn sneakers slipped on wet, browned pine needles, and she grasped tree trunks to keep from falling, while dew dripped on her from the interlaced canopy of needles and leaves. Below the canopy, everything was brown except for a few green seedlings on their way up to form new trees. Lyn felt as if she were climbing in a damp cave.

"Isn't it beautiful? Oh, it smells so wonderful," Mrs. Maclean exulted behind her.

Lyn mistrusted Mrs. Maclean's enthusiasm this morning. It seemed fake.

They kept climbing. Dad pointed out a trout lily with its green and white leaves and delicate yellow flower. Brian caught a toad and tried to slip it into Lyn's sweat shirt pocket. She pushed him away, and they had a mock battle on the slippery path, with Brian ducking and begging for mercy in the midst of his laughter. Burlap bounced around, barking at them both, while Mrs. Maclean shrilled, "Don't upset that dog. He'll attack you."

There wasn't enough room for a proper battle, anyway. After Brian tripped and fell backward over Burlap, they called a truce, grinning at each other while Burlap licked Brian's face, then evened things up by licking Lyn's.

"So there," Lyn said, claiming victory in their tussle by virtue of being upright. Brian stood and brushed off his rear end.

They didn't find the waterfall. Brian said they must have taken the wrong fork. When they reached a lookout point with a view, Dad and Mrs. Maclean decided they'd had enough climbing for a while and sat down to rest.

"Let's see if we can locate that waterfall," Brian said to Lyn.

She hesitated about leaving their parents alone,

but asked herself how much harm five minutes could do and finally set off with Brian and Burlap to retrace their steps to the fork.

The nearest thing to a waterfall was a trickle of water coming down between rocks. "Could this be it?" Brian asked.

"Maybe it was bigger when they laid out the trail," Lyn said charitably.

Somehow in returning to the lookout point, they strayed onto a different path and came out at a crossroads in the park, instead of where their parents were waiting for them.

"Left," Brian said.

"Listen, I know you're a Boy Scout and all that, but Burlap seems to want to go right."

"You trust a dog more than me?" Brian asked in mock dismay.

"Well, he's got instincts. And you're only human."

"No way I'm going to argue that one." Brian detached the leash from the dog's collar and said, "Lead on, Burpie."

They walked down the road. The mist had lifted finally. Suddenly Lyn said, "We left them alone again, didn't we?"

"You worry too much," Brian said. "I asked my mother flat out last night how she felt about your father. She said she only likes him as a friend. What she's after is a master's in social work. That's all. But she warned me that if my father won't budge, she's going to Boston without him. I'm the one facing a breakup, not you."

"You're sure that's the truth? I mean, what she said about my father?"

Brian stiffened.

"I'm sorry, but you said yourself she tells white lies."

"That wouldn't be a white lie—it'd be a whopper," Brian said. "I asked her straight and she answered me straight."

"Well," Lyn said, "I hope your parents don't separate, but you know what? If your father stays, then you wouldn't have to move, and you'd keep Burlap."

"She wants me to go with her whatever happens," he said quietly.

"And you will?"

Brian gave his shrug. Lyn felt sorry for him. There didn't seem to be any good alternatives for him. "Anyway, she is fun to be with."

"Yeah. She's okay."

Burlap returned from exploring the brush and wagged his tail for attention. "You sure you're leading us home, Burpie?" Lyn asked, using Brian's diminutive. Burlap sat down in the road facing them. "Home, back to the campsites," Lyn told him. "Come on, show us the way." He picked up a paw, set it down and tried the other one as if he was more than willing to oblige, if he only knew how.

"Maybe he hasn't got a sense of direction," Brian suggested. "After all, nobody's perfect, not even Burlap."

Burlap watched a noisy blue jay in the tree over his head, then got up to urinate on some ferns. He seemed content to be wherever they were, wherever that was.

"I should've brought my compass," Brian mumbled.

A car whizzed by them. "Let's stop a car and ask directions," Lyn said. "Left may have been right, after all. We should be someplace we recognize by now, shouldn't we?"

"Well, we're on a road, and it's got to go somewhere."

They kept walking, taking in the sweet grass smell and lyric bird calls of the newly minted morning while they waited for a slow-moving car to hail. Brian tugged her braid and pretended innocence when she whipped around to look at him.

"Try that again and I'll deck you," she threatened, and surprised herself by saying, "I'm thinking of cutting it."

"Your braid? How come?"

"It's a pain to take care of. Besides, I'm tired of it."

"But your father said—"

"My father doesn't give me any say in his personal life. So why should I care how he feels about my hair. My hair is *my* personal business."

"You mad at him?"

"I guess so. I keep getting suspicious that they planned this weekend. I mean, to end up here without Dora or your father around." She waited for his shrug and it came. "That doesn't make you angry?"

"All I care about is that my folks stay together," he said.

"And what about Burlap?"

He shrugged more hopelessly.

It had gotten so warm and sunny that they were perspiring by the time they saw the farmhouse and realized they'd walked clear out of the park. "Let's go ask those people for directions," Lyn said.

"What people? Nobody's around, and the place is plastered with BAD DOG and NO TRESPASSING signs."

"A holiday morning in the country? Where would they be but home? I'm going to check," Lyn insisted.

He hung back, but she marched ahead. With some hesitation, Burlap followed her. The house was a plain white-shingled box overshadowed by the red barn and silo beside it. A field with newly sprouted plants in even rows stretched out on the other side. Lyn opened the gate in the barbed-wire fence surrounding the place. She walked up the driveway to the farmhouse. Dogs began to bark, first one and then another.

"You better come back," Brian called nervously.

"They're probably tied up," Lyn said, and kept going toward the house. She expected the barking to bring whoever lived there to the front door. A car was parked beside the house. Someone must be home.

"Lyn, please come back!" Brian called.

She halted as the first dog rounded the building and came charging right for her. It was long-haired, black and medium-sized. Right behind it was a hound, and to join the cacophony, a large old collie with a year's worth of burrs embedded in its matted fur loped around the last corner. All three dogs revved up their noise level, preparing for action.

Lyn couldn't decide whether to turn and run now or to stand her ground and hope they wouldn't attack. No question they could beat her in a race to the gate. The black dog stopped a few feet away and snarled up at her, teeth bared. It was crouching to jump just as Burlap shoved in front of her.

"Now run, Lyn," Brian yelled.

She fled. As soon as she was safe outside the gate, Brian called to Burlap to come. But he was in the middle of a snapping lunge and parry fight. While he and the aggressive black dog threatened each other and maneuvered for the best position, the collie went for his flank and the hound lunged for his back leg. Suddenly there was a tumbling mass of dogs, all barking and howling and making an unearthly racket.

"We've got to do something," Lyn said. She grabbed a rock from the side of the road and ran back inside. Brian picked up a stone, too. He threw it and hit the hound, who went yelping back to the house. The door flew open, and an old man yelled at them.

"You leave them dogs alone."

"They're attacking us," Lyn said. "I was just coming to ask for directions, and they attacked me."

"Can't you read? You get out of here before I call the police on you. You're *trespassing*." His emphasis made the word sound like a major criminal offense.

The collie had halted at the sound of the old man's voice. Now it ran up to the front steps of the house, wagging its tail. The black dog stood its ground, growling meanly. Brian said, "Come, Burlap," and walked away. The black dog lunged and bit at Burlap's shoulder as he turned to follow Brian and Lyn, who was backing toward the road, too.

Burlap swung around. A deep, menacing growl issued from his throat. *Now* he was angry, the growl meant, and the black dog fled with its tail between its legs.

Outside the fence, they stopped to look Burlap over. "He doesn't seem to be badly hurt," Brian said. "I don't see any blood on his shoulder or anywhere. Good thing his fur's so thick."

"I could have gotten him killed," Lyn said. "He saved me."

A pickup truck driven by a long-haired young man with sleepy eyes stopped. "You kids got a problem?"

"We're lost," Lyn said. When she told him where they wanted to go, he said they were only half a mile or so off course and gave them directions.

"Want a lift?"

"No, thanks," Brian said. "We can walk it."

"Suit yourself." The young man spun his wheels as he took off.

"We could have gotten there a lot faster in the truck," Lyn said when it was gone.

"Haven't you gotten in enough trouble being trusting today?"

"But he was nice."

"Yeah, and the farm looked nice, too, right?"

He had made his point. Lyn changed the subject. "Burlap was wonderful, wasn't he?"

"He saved you, all right."

She bent down and kissed the dog's tipped-over ear flap. Burlap looked up at her fondly, as calm as if he'd already forgotten the fight. They walked the half-mile back into the park in companionable silence.

"Wait till they hear what happened to us," Lyn said when she finally saw her father's car gleaming in the sunlight at the campsite.

"I hope they haven't got half the park out looking for us," Brian said.

Nobody was waiting for them at the campsite. Burlap took himself into the lake for an impromptu swim.

"I wouldn't mind joining him," Lyn said. "Dad'll want to leave after lunch. We could squeeze in a swim. How about it?"

"First, we better let our folks know we're okay," Brian said.

"Sure. Why don't you see if they're at your campsite, and if they're not, leave a note and get on your suit and come back here. Meanwhile, I'll hike up to the lookout just in case they're still waiting."

"They're not going to be up there in the woods, not this long."

"So where should I look?" Lyn asked.

"Let me check my camp first, and we'll think about it." He set off down the road. Burlap climbed out of the water and shook himself, then lay down on the warm stone. Lyn was pleased that even though he wasn't on a leash, he hadn't tried to follow Brian.

"Good dog," she said, and crawled into the tent to change into her suit.

When she came back out, she heard Mrs.

Maclean's low laugh and Dad's chuckle. If they were worried about their children's disappearance, they didn't sound it. They had stopped in the road. Lyn could just see them through the long branches of the pine tree that marked the entrance to the campsite. The tent obstructed their view of her. Lyn went cold and then hot as she watched their bodies tangle in a kiss. She'd sat through enough love stories on TV and in the movies to recognize passion when she saw it. Rage shook her as she stood there watching them.

She was lying on her sleeping bag in the tent in tears when her father found her. "Lyn, baby, what's the matter? We got a little lost; so we're late getting back, but nothing happened."

"Go away," she said. "Leave me alone."

"She's very upset," she heard him tell Brian a minute later. "I guess she must have thought something happened to us."

"Maybe it's a delayed reaction to what happened to her," Brian said. Briefly, he retold their experience with the farm dogs.

Lyn couldn't lie there forever, hating her father. She got up and, even though she felt sick to her stomach, rolled up her sleeping bag and gathered her possessions. By the time she went back outside, Brian had gone.

"You feeling better?" Dad asked.

"No."

"Well, I made a few sandwiches. Want to eat them on the road?"

"Yes, let's get home."

Dad looked at her with concern and said sympathetically, "You sit in the sun while I pack the car. That must have been one terrifying experience with those dogs."

She let him think that was what was wrong because she wasn't ready to leap into accusations about what was. While he worked, she tried to think about what she would say to him in the car going home, but her brain wasn't operating. She ate one of the sandwiches to regain the energy she'd lost, and the food did help some. By the time they drove off, she felt calmer.

"Want to talk about it?" he asked gently after he turned onto the main road.

"Not really." What she wanted was to confront him with what she'd seen, but she held back. She couldn't stand it if he lied. Maybe she couldn't stand a confession, either.

Lyn thought about Dora. Dora was the one Dad was betraying the worst. Lyn had to warn her. Or did Dora already know? Once before in her life, Lyn remembered feeling this confused and helpless. It was after her mother died, but she'd had her father to turn to then. Now she had no one. What irked her most was that she couldn't understand how she could have misjudged her father so badly that she'd trusted him to do what was right. Why hadn't she seen that all he really cared about was himself?

Dad reached past Burlap to pat her hand, still thinking she was upset about the dogs' attack. Lyn jerked her hands away. "Lyn?" he questioned.

"Leave me alone," she told him.

He looked at her anxiously and then he did.

TWELVE

Burlap set a heavy paw on Lyn's leg to claim her attention. She patted him, and he hunkered down on the car seat, laying both front paws and his head in her lap, which was the most of him that would fit. The green woods spooled past them as Lyn watched mindlessly. All she had to say was, "Dad, I saw you kiss Mrs. Maclean," but she couldn't get the words out. She couldn't even think them without wincing inside.

They were off the highway and nearly home before Dad said, "You're awfully quiet. I wish you'd talk about those dogs."

"I'm not upset about the dogs."

"You're not? What then?"

She shook her head. The words were a tight ball in her chest.

"I'd say the weekend was a big success," he said, and glanced at her questioningly.

"The first part was," she agreed.

"And you did like Sylvia, didn't you?"

He'd hit a nerve and Lyn snapped, "Not much."

He raised his eyebrows and let the conversation drop.

They got home to find the driveway jammed with the cars of people there to claim their dogs.

"Could you two give me a hand?" Dora called to them apologetically when they got out of the car, which Dad had parked on the road. Helping Dora was a welcome diversion. Dad took over the office procedures, and Lyn retrieved people's dogs from the kennel. By the time the rush was over, and they'd unloaded the car and eaten supper, it was late.

"How was the weekend?" Dora asked.

"We ran into Brian and his mother at the campsite and joined forces with them," Dad said. "Did some canoeing and hiking. Lyn had a bad experience at the end, though." He looked at Lyn sympathetically.

Dora was looking at her, too. Lyn shut her eyes against the image of her father embracing Sylvia Maclean.

"I'm very tired. I think I'll go to bed now," Lyn murmured. She put her arms around Dora and hugged her, reluctant to let go, until Dora began to fidget and pushed her lightly away.

Lyn heard their voices as she trudged upstairs. Dora asked what had happened, and Dad related the incident with the farm dogs as Brian had told it to him. Burlap's nails clicked on the stairs as he followed Lyn up. Tomorrow, she told herself, after a good night's sleep, she'd be strong enough to have it out with Dad. Tomorrow she'd confront him with his betrayal, his deceit. Then she would demand to know what he really intended to do with their lives.

In bed Lyn closed her eyes and saw the pines still rolling past the car window, the trickle of waterfall, the island where they had swum. Finally, she fell asleep.

"You feeling better this morning?" Dora asked, when Lyn and she were alone in the kitchen the next morning.

"I'm okay."

"Something happened between your father and her, didn't it?"

Lyn burst into tears. Dora said comfortingly, "Don't worry, Lyn. You'll come out all right."

"But what about you, Dora? What about you?"

"I'll be okay. I knew all along that it wouldn't last."

"Then why did you marry him?"

"Because he asked me, and I thought, why not if he wanted me. And it's lasted three years."

"But Dora, he married you forever. He's your husband."

Dora gave a wry smile.

Lyn asked, "Don't you love him?"

"He's not happy with me."

"Not happy? What do you mean he's not happy? Why shouldn't he be? Please, don't sit back and let Mrs. Maclean take him away from you. Please, Dora."

"She couldn't take him if he didn't want to go." Dora's eyes were compassionate, as if she felt sorrier for Lyn than for herself. "Lyn," she said, "whatever happens between your father and me, if you need me, I'll be there."

Despairing, Lyn watched her stepmother collect the breakfast dishes and take them to the sink. For Dora, it was settled. Whatever Dad decided was how it would be.

In school, Jen took one look at Lyn and asked her what was wrong. Even Shelly noticed and stopped gushing about her weekend movie date long enough to inquire if Lyn was feeling sick or something.

"I'm fine," Lyn told her. "Tell me more about the movie." And Shelly did.

Lyn walked by her father, who was on hall duty during change of classes. A girl who still had a crush on him this late in the year was hanging on his arm, trying to talk him into something. Dad winked at Lyn, but she passed by as if he were a stranger.

Brian sat next to her on the bus going home. "So," he began confidentially, "I shook my mother up. I told her if Dad doesn't go to Boston with her, I'm staying here to keep him company."

"Brian! You said that?"

"Well, it makes sense, doesn't it? She can get what she wants, but she can't have it all." He looked fierce as his eyes met Lyn's.

"What did she say?"

"Nothing. She kind of gasped and went away. I'll hear plenty when she's thought it over, believe me."

"I'm impressed," Lyn said. "I haven't even told my father—" She stopped, remembering Brian didn't know what she'd seen. And how could she tell him that his mother had exchanged a passionate embrace with a man to whom she wasn't married? It was too shameful.

A letter addressed to her father was in the mail that Wednesday. Normally, Lyn wouldn't have paid any attention to it, but the return address was Boston. She asked Dad about it when he drove her to school the next morning.

"It was from my friend Tom."

"The one who got a job as principal of a middle school in Boston?"

"Right."

She braced herself. "What did he have to say?"

"He offered me a job in his school next fall if I want it."

"You've already asked him about a job?"

"I just wanted to see what he'd say. I haven't made any decisions yet."

"Well, I've made a decision," Lyn said angrily. "I like it here. And I'm staying, whether you do or not." She slammed the car door shut behind her and ran into the school.

Shelly had a new haircut that drew a lot of compliments that morning. A friend of her sister's had done it, Shelly said. "She's really a great stylist, and she barely charges anything because she's just starting out."

"Do me a favor," Lyn said, "and ask her if she'll cut my hair."

"Your hair?" Shelly's eyes widened. "You wouldn't!"

"See if she can do it Monday. Monday after school would be good for me." Just saying it made Lyn feel better, as if she were in control of her own life instead of being totally at her father's mercy.

"You'll change your mind by Monday, I bet," Shelly said. Doubtfully, she added, "Won't you?"

Half an hour later, Jen came rushing up to Lyn in the library. "Is it true? Shelly says you're going to get your braid cut off."

"So? I can if I want to. It's my hair."

"But without your braid, how will I know who you are?"

"Jen, will you come to the beauty parlor with me? I need someone to hold my hand in case I get scared." Lyn tried to smile. "And then you'll see the before and after me."

"You'll look grown up without your braid," Jen said reproachfully.

"I hope so." To be grown up was what she wanted. Nothing was worse than being a dependent child. All day Lyn felt better.

Burlap was sleeping on the rug next to her bed. When Lyn awoke at three in the morning and tried to remember her mother, Burlap was in the middle of a dream. His legs ran as he whimpered in his sleep.

It seemed to Lyn that she could remember her mother's lilting laugh and that she'd been a woman who laughed easily. Dora was sad and passive, but still she was Mother now. Dora was Mother, and no other woman ever would be, not even one who might fill the role better. "If you need me, I'll be there," Dora had promised. Well, Lyn needed her.

Dora would let her stay. Dad could move to Boston if he liked, chase after Mrs. Maclean if he wanted. Lyn would stay here where she fitted so snugly.

In the morning Burlap woke Lyn up by pressing the tip of his cold, spongy, black nose against her arm. He looked apologetic about it and did his eager little two-step, absurdly dainty for so large a dog, by way of asking her to let him out.

"Okay," she told him. "I'll get dressed and walk you. Hang on a minute." Burlap had been doting on her more since the camping trip. Lyn wondered if rescuing her from the farm dogs had made her more important to him.

Returning from the walk, Lyn saw Dora outside exercising an arthritic Saint Bernard. The owner had asked Dora to force the dog to walk to keep his stiffening joints mobile. Dora was clucking encouragement at the drooling, sad-eyed beast. "Come on, Elmo," she coaxed, and he rose with a strangely human moan and moved a couple of feet before collapsing to the ground again.

"That poor dog!" Lyn said. "Can't you just let him be?"

"It wouldn't be doing him a favor," Dora said.

Lyn wished Dora were as determined about her own life as she was in dealing with animals. "Did you know Dad's thinking of taking a job in Boston?"

"Yes, I know," Dora said quietly.

"Well, so what did you tell him about it?"

"Nothing. It's his decision."

"His decision? But it's going to change all our lives, Dora."

"I can't help that," Dora said, and turned her attention back to the Saint Bernard.

Monday was the first day of Spirit Week. Lyn wore purple kneesocks and a shirt with purple violets printed on it.

"You're sure you want to go through with this?" Jen asked anxiously after school, when the three of them were walking toward the beauty parlor and the scissors of Shelly's sister's friend.

"Positive," Lyn said. She was nervous but determined as they opened the garish pink and blue door of the hair salon.

"Isn't this exciting?" Shelly said. "I bet Lyn's going to look fabulous in short hair."

"Not short, shorter," Lyn said. "Maybe shoulder length. I don't want my head flying off without any hair to anchor it."

"I wish you'd talked this over with your father or your stepmother," Jen fretted. "Something as big as this needs talking over."

"It's my hair," Lyn said stubbornly.

Normally the salon was closed on Mondays, but a spiky-haired young woman in a short skirt was sitting in a chair all alone in the empty place, waiting for them.

"Fay?" Lyn quavered, her stomach suddenly knotting.

"Hi. So you're the kid with the braid." She eyed it speculatively. "You sure you want it chopped off?"

Lyn barely had the strength to nod.

"Well, you look through that book of hairstyles

there and pick one," Fay said. "You guys can help her. This is a big decision."

The three girls dropped in a row onto the red plastic chairs next to the cocktail table and began flipping through the looseleaf book that lay on it. Cold terror kept Lyn from taking in the hairstyles. She listened to Shelly's comments until Jen said, "How about this? It's shoulder length and it'd look good on you."

"But it's not pizzazzy," Shelly said.

"It's pizzazzy enough for Lyn."

"She'd look nice with that simple cut," Fay agreed. "It's better not to go too extreme the first time. We don't want her not recognizing herself in the mirror."

"Right," Lyn croaked. "I'll go with that one." She put herself in Fay's hands and closed her eyes.

"First I'll chomp off the tail," Fay said. "Then we'll wash and cut the rest. Okay?"

Fay chattered as she led Lyn to the chair and tied a cape around her. "So how come you three are all wearing purple? Funeral for the braid?" Fay laughed at her own joke.

"No, it's Spirit Week at school. Today's purple day," Shelly told her. Shelly had a purple streak in her hair and a purple scarf around her hips. Jen was wearing a purple smock.

Fay wanted to know all about Spirit Week. "Lyn started it," Shelly said. "You should see. Most of the kids wore something purple today, and getting most of the kids in our school to do anything is a miracle."

"They're not even going to recognize you when you walk in tomorrow without your braid," Jen said.

"Shut up, Jen," Shelly said. "You're making her nervous."

Lyn hoped Fay would hurry. She thought she might faint if she had to wait much longer.

The braid was hard to hack off. "Sorry to be amputating without anesthetic," Fay joked. No one said anything. Even Shelly looked anxious.

Finally Fay said, "There we go," and held up the tail for Lyn's inspection. "You keep this. You can always use it as a hairpiece, and if you ever want to wear a braid again, I could pin it on for you."

"Uh." Lyn looked in wide-eyed horror at her dead braid. She recoiled when Fay dropped it into her lap and was glad to close her eyes again during the hair washing. Shelly began chattering about some TV show she'd seen. The scissors snipped and snipped until Lyn became certain she was going to wind up bald. She thought of a picture she'd seen of women who'd collaborated with the enemy during World War II, whose hair had been cut off as punishment. Finally, Fay whirled her chair around to face the mirror.

"So what do you think?"

Lyn saw a girl with a flounce of shoulder-length blond hair and a frightened face. "That's me?" she asked.

"You look pretty!" Jen said in surprise.

"Ooo, I love it," Shelly said. "Don't you love it, Lyn?"

"Yeah, I think it came out good," Fay said with satisfaction.

Lyn stood up shakily, still looking at the girl in the mirror. Her head felt strange without the weight of the braid, dizzy and light, and, yes, she did look—interesting now, older, more feminine, more something different.

Dora came in from feeding the dogs, looked at Lyn and asked, "Do you like it?"

"Yes," Lyn said defiantly.

Dora nodded. "Well, good for you," she said, and went to the sink to wash her hands.

"So you did it. You *cut* it," Brian said when he delivered Burlap to her door. He stared open-mouthed at Lyn.

"So?" She faced him boldly.

His lip twitched and he dropped his eyes. "It looks good."

"But what?"

"But I wish I'd had a camera when you were drying it on the island." He blushed and changed the subject quickly. "Well, I'll see you tomorrow. You better like my hat!"

She was alone in the kitchen with tears trickling down her cheeks when her father walked in. Burlap was stretched out near the table. Cinder was tucked under his chin. The big dog didn't move, but his tail thumped in acknowledgment of Dad's entry.

"So," Dad said, "the consensus is Spirit Week's gotten off to a good start. I understand even Miss Mackay wore a purple dress."

"She was the most purple teacher of all."

He was removing his purple tie from his lavender shirt as he spoke. Suddenly his fingers froze on the knot. "Lyn! What'd you do to yourself?"

"Doesn't it look good, Dad?"

"But—" The tears that filled his eyes amazed Lyn. "How could you cut your braid without even asking me?"

"You applied for a job in Boston without asking me."

"So you punished me?"

"And," she continued, finally letting it all drain out of her, "on our big camp-out, you pretended you wanted to spend time alone with me, but you really wanted to be with Mrs. Maclean. I don't know if you planned it that way from the start, but that's how it worked out. And"—she took a deep breath and released the words with it—"I saw you kissing her."

"Oh," he said. "So that's what hit you."

"Is that all you can say?" Lyn asked hysterically.

"Lyn." He halted, for the first time ever at a loss for words. "I can imagine how you—it's too bad you happened to see us. Actually, we didn't mean to touch each other. It just happened. It was an accident."

"An accident? But you're still going to Boston, and she's going, too. Right?"

He winced and said, "We'll talk later, when you've calmed down."

"I'm calm."

"Well, I'm not." He turned and walked out of the room.

It didn't matter what he said, anyway, she thought. He couldn't explain away his actions. She might not stop loving him altogether, but she wasn't craning her neck looking up to him now. He'd crashed off the pedestal. It was like the change in her hairstyle: easier but not special anymore, and it made her feel awful.

THIRTEEN

Tuesday was hat day. Lyn felt so little like going to school wearing some kind of silly hat that she considered staying home and playing hooky for the first time in her life. It didn't help that a shiny blue morning awaited her outside. Rain would have suited her mood better. Burlap nudged her hopefully. She padded downstairs in her pajamas and let him into the exercise yard before climbing back up to search for hats. Neither she nor Dora wore any, but Dad was partial to them and had an extensive collection in his closet. Lyn was thinking about his Greek fisherman's hat when he came out of his room wearing it. "How do I look?" he asked.

"Fine. Do you have another hat I could borrow?"

"You're welcome to anything on the shelf. Listen, daughter of mine, after school today, you and I have to talk."

She tensed. "About what?"

"Not now. I'm already late."

As he ran down the stairs, she stood in the doorway chewing on her lip, before resolutely shoving the worry about what he might have to tell her out of her mind. It couldn't be worse than what she already expected, and right now she had a more immediate problem—what to put on her head.

Dad looked good in hats, which was probably why he liked them. He had several short-brimmed, high-crowned models in his closet: one Tyrolean-style for the winter, one plaid wool, a straw with a broader brim. Lyn tried that on, but it didn't become her. Neither did the baseball-type cap or the woolen ski helmet. She didn't want to appear in school without her braid for the first time looking ridiculous. A flat-top sports cap with a short bill made her look tough. Not too bad, she decided as she eyed herself in the mirror.

"Hat day?" Dora asked when Lyn got downstairs. Dora wrinkled her nose at the cap. "I have a straw hat with flowers you could borrow."

"That's your wedding hat!"

"Well, I'll never wear it again. I only bought the fool thing because I wasn't getting a real wedding dress." Dora looked off into space. "I wish we'd taken pictures, though."

The sadness in her voice made Lyn say, "Oh, Dora, I remember how you looked. You looked beautiful."

"Almost. Anyway, they say all brides are beautiful."

"Dora, I wanted to ask you. If Dad goes to Boston, would you mind—I mean, would it matter to you if I stayed here with you?"

"Sure, you can stay," Dora said quickly. "I told you, if you need me. . . . I don't think your father will agree to it, though. Have you asked him?"

"Not yet," Lyn said.

"Well, see what he says," Dora said, and walked out the back door.

Lyn was disappointed. Now was the time she needed to hear Dora say something about feeling like her mother or about love. True, it was hard for Dora to express emotion, and Lyn understood that, but she was afraid that whether she stayed or went wouldn't really matter all that much to Dora. To be welcome, but not loved—was that enough?

Lyn glanced at the clock and gasped. Burlap would have to do without his walk this morning. She grabbed a muffin and a banana and dashed to the bus stop, where Brian was already waiting.

"What do you think of my hat?" Brian asked her with an expectant grin.

She thought it was goofy, full of fishing lures that looked like bugs or shiny bits of metal tacked on a shapeless bowl with a shapeless brim. "It has character," she said tactfully.

He chuckled and told her, "Women never understand fishing hats. This one's a beaut. It was my grandfather's. He always took me fishing when I visited, even in the winter, even in the rain, and he always caught something. He's the one taught me to like fishing."

"I could show you a bridge over a creek near here where people fish," Lyn offered.

"Sure," he said. "That'd be good. If—"

"If what?"

His light brown eyes darkened. "If I'm still around. My mother's been hammering hard on me about not going to Boston with her."

"You won't give in, will you?"

"No. My dad was really pleased that I'm staying with him. He got all choked up and told me I was a good son." Brian smiled and shrugged.

"I wonder what my father will say if I tell him I'm staying with Dora," Lyn said dreamily.

"But you can't. Dora's just your stepmother."

"She's as much my mother as anyone will ever be."

"Well, it'd be nice if we both stayed," Brian offered. "Then nothing would have to change except we'd take the bus to high school next fall."

"Nothing?" she asked. "What about you wouldn't have a mother around and I wouldn't have a father?"

"I think I'd hate that less than moving to an old city with streets full of garbage where I don't know a soul."

She wondered how she'd feel without her father. He was such a constant, it was impossible to imagine life without him—such a constant that she could only assume she loved him without having any measure of how much. "Do I look really gross in Dad's cap?" she asked Brian.

He made a face. "It doesn't do a whole lot for you. I mean—"

"I know what you mean. Never mind." She'd get the day over with and handle that talk with her father when the time came for it. She ate the muffin she was still holding after Brian refused her offer to share it.

The school bus whined to a halt ahead of them and they climbed aboard.

"The braid, where's the braid?" Boy Johnson howled when he saw Lyn in the hall. Half the eighth grade stopped to turn around and stare at her as the tall boy pointed in horror. "What'd you do with it?"

"Cut it off," Lyn said, explaining the obvious.

"It's Lyn!" a girl she barely knew exclaimed. "I walked right by without recognizing you."

"I like your hat," Jen said, coming up beside her. She had on a tam that suited her small, plain face.

"That braid was a permanent institution in our lives," Boy Johnson yelled. "How could you just lop it off without warning us? The shock is too much." He staggered down the hall in his ten-gallon hat, holding his hand over his heart like a cowboy who'd been shot. Snickers followed his performance.

The rest of the commentary on her braidlessness was mild compared to Boy Johnson's. Girls claimed to like the new hairdo. Boys made comments like, "You've lost your tail!" or "Hey, Lyn, is that you?"

A few weeks ago all the brouhaha would have shaken her, but today it barely touched her. A hairstyle just didn't rate on the scale of her present concerns.

Lyn was on her way to the girls' room after lunch when she saw her father and Mr. Hoot coming out of the faculty lounge together. The social studies teacher had his arm draped across her father's shoulders. Lyn heard Mr. Hoot say confidentially, "Saw you with your lady friend Friday, and let me tell you, I don't blame you, Bruce. She's some looker."

Dad shrugged off the arm with a muttered comment. His eyes met Lyn's and squeezed as if he were pained.

"Hi, Lyn," Mr. Hoot said. "I like your hat."

She ignored him and walked into the girls' room to escape them both. Last Friday, she thought, as she stood at the wash basin letting the water run over her hands. Where had Dad been on Friday? Somewhere with Mrs. Maclean if Hoot had seen them. Dad was shameless. His conscience had simply shut down. She stood at the sink, hurting too much to move. She missed the pride she'd had in him, her honorable father who was a teacher because that was where he could contribute most to society even if the pay was modest, her good, decent, honest father whom everyone respected. Dora might not care more about her than about any other stray, but it would be better to stay with Dora than go to Boston with him just so that he could be with Mrs. Maclean.

Lyn turned the faucet off and stood dripping water on the floor without reaching for the paper towels. It had struck her that if Mrs. Maclean were going to be part of Dad's life, Burlap wouldn't be. Taking Burlap to Boston wasn't the greatest idea, anyway. He'd have a hard time getting used to city streets, and in cities, apartments were small. Even houses were small. Another reason to stay with Dora.

"There you are," Shelly said, bursting into the bathroom. "I've been looking all over for you." She frowned at Lyn. "What's wrong? Someone say something mean about your braid?"

Lyn shook her head.

"Well, what is it, then?"

"I can't tell you, Shelly."

"Why? Aren't I your best friend?"

"Please," she begged, and began crying.

"Lyn," Shelly said solemnly, "I never saw *you* cry. It must be what people are saying about your father."

"What are people saying about him?" Alarm dried the tears in an instant.

"Well, you know, about that woman, Brian's mother, and him."

"*Everybody* knows?"

"Not everybody. And don't blame me. I didn't say a word, even though I saw them in the parking lot when I was coming out of the bowling alley. They were holding hands and making eyes at each other. You know."

Lyn put her wet hands over her ears. "No," she said. "No."

Shelly was hurt. "Well, I'm just telling you what I *saw*, Lyn."

Lyn bolted for a stall because she felt like throwing up, but then she couldn't. Instead, she stood behind the door, crying again.

"Lyn." Shelly knocked on the door. "Listen, don't feel bad. He can't help falling in love. Nobody can.

And falling in love makes you crazy, believe you me."
The bell rang for the next class. "Uh-oh," Shelly said.
"Late again."

"I've got to get to gym." Lyn rushed out ahead of
Shelly, who meant well but wasn't the person to comfort her now.

"Listen," Brian said as they were leaving the last class
of the day, "my mother's taking me to a dentist
appointment after school. Could you walk Burlap
for me today?"

"No problem." Adults had strange priorities, Lyn
thought. Mrs. Maclean might be leaving her husband for her next-door neighbor, but not before she
attended to her son's dental care.

Dad was waiting for Lyn in his car. "How about
going to an ice cream parlor for our talk," he suggested.

"I have to walk Burlap for Brian. You could walk
with me if you want."

"Fine." Dad wasn't smiling and he sounded grim.

Burlap's tail whacked a welcome against the floor
while his big body shuddered in delight when they
walked into the kitchen. Lyn knelt and kissed his
long nose. Dora was playing solitaire in the dining
room.

"We're taking Burlap for a walk," Dad told her,
and asked politely, "Need anything before we go?"

"No," Dora said, "not a thing." The curtain of hair
hid her face as she bent her head to the cards.

Lyn led the way up the hill where Brian had

showed her the sunset. A faint haylike odor from the warmed grass hung in the light spring air. Burlap began nosing eagerly around after the scent of rabbits or mice or fox or some other interesting creature.

"Think how different the world would be if you experienced it through your nose," Dad said.

"Umm." Lyn was trying to decide how to talk to him about staying with Dora. She didn't know whether the subject made her so uneasy because she was afraid of his reaction or because she wasn't sure she really wanted to stay

A horse trailer rumbled by. Two swishing tails hung out the open back, attached to smooth, horseshoe-shaped brown rumps. Then came a lady with a carload of children. Burlap dropped a stick at Lyn's feet, looking up at her hopefully. She threw the stick, and he galloped after it.

"I don't know quite how to start, Lyn," Dad said. "But I want you to know that you've hurt me. You've misjudged me and been quick to believe the worst. I expected you to have more faith in your father."

Lyn was startled. He was accusing her of hurting him, but she was the one who was hurting. "Dad," she said, "I'm not making judgments. You taught me that promises should be kept, and you're not keeping yours to Dora."

"But I am."

"Dad!"

"I don't care what people think or say, Lyn, or what you think you saw. I can't help how strongly I feel about Sylvia, but I haven't done anything besides kiss her once and talk to her. That does not constitute infidelity, certainly not by modern standards."

Lyn thought about it. She wanted to believe him, to trust him again even at the price of being ashamed of herself for having doubted him. "Okay," Lyn said. "I'm glad. I'd hate it if I couldn't respect you."

"Well, then—"

"But you see her alone sometimes when Dora doesn't know."

"Yes. That's true. I don't like making Dora unhappy. It upsets her that Sylvia and I communicate so well, and so I don't broadcast every meeting."

"That's not honest, Dad."

"Sometimes being too honest is hurtful to people. Dora knows I'm not happy with her. I haven't deceived her about that."

"Are you going to divorce her?"

"I don't know."

"Well, are you taking that job in Boston?"

He nodded. "I'd like to, which is part of why I wanted to talk to you. How will you feel about moving to Boston?"

"I'm not moving."

He made a gesture of impatience. "Lyn, that doesn't sound like you. You've always made the best of things. You're a yea-sayer. You'd like it once you were there. Boston has many advantages: the museums and theater and—there're beaches nearby."

"I'd hate it because I don't want to leave Dora or my friends or my school or this neighborhood. And what about Burlap? I'd have to leave him behind, too, wouldn't I? You'd get a new job and Mrs. Maclean, Dad, but all I'd do is lose."

"Then what do you expect me to do? Give up everything and stay here?"

"What do you expect me to do? Give up everything and go?"

"I want to take that job in Boston," Dad said. "I'm getting to an age where there aren't a whole lot of chances for a new start. While for you, everything's still possible. That's why I'm asking *you* to make the sacrifice." His voice became wheedling. "We wouldn't be leaving until midsummer, and you could come back and visit often."

"Dora says I'm welcome to stay with her if you agree."

His eyes probed to see if she was bluffing. "You wouldn't do that to me, would you?"

"You'd have Mrs. Maclean. Dora wouldn't have anybody."

"She'd have her dogs. She'd have this place. Dora's a solitary sort of person. She doesn't need you. I do."

Lyn caught her breath. He had never in her entire life told her that he needed her. "Dad!" she said, and then she remembered. "But what about Mrs. Maclean?"

"I don't know. I'm not certain that Sylvia and I are— The reason I haven't discussed things with you all along is I don't know what to tell you exactly. But I'm too old and cautious to go leaping from one relationship to another without a time gap. So you needn't worry for a long time. I'm going to Boston because I want a change of life-style, not because of Sylvia. I'm just not built to be a country boy."

Burlap barked at a rock with a hole at the base where some animal lived. "And what about Burlap?" Lyn asked.

Dad looked at the big dog for a minute. Then he said, "We'll work something out."

"Like what?"

"You can take him with you. That much I can do for you. I'll find a place big enough for the three of us somehow. Okay?"

She closed her eyes. "I have to think about it," she said.

They returned from the walk just as Brian and his mother were turning into their driveway. Mrs. Maclean stopped the car and called, "Lyn, when did you cut your hair?"

Lyn touched her head. "Yesterday." She'd forgotten about the braid.

"I can't believe it! Come here and let me look at you."

Lyn approached the car warily. Mrs. Maclean appraised the hairdo with a proprietary interest.

"I like it. It's much softer and more feminine but— whatever made you do it?" She sounded as if she had a right to know, as if she were already Lyn's mother.

"I just got sick of the braid," Lyn said. She ducked away from the intimate scrutiny, said, "Excuse me," and hurried toward the house.

FOURTEEN

Lyn couldn't wait for international day to be over. She kept thinking about Boston and her father and Dora and wondering what to do. The high-backed comb that was supposed to complete her Spanish señorita costume kept slipping out of her hair, or else her embroidered shawl was slipping off her shoulders. Jen did better with the six yards of gauzy cotton that Lyn had turned into a sari for her in the girls' room. People complimented Jen on the sari, even asking if her parents had come from India. Jen finally started claiming that her maternal grand-mother had been a maharajah. Brian heard her and told Lyn to tell Jen a grandmother would be a maha-rani. Maharajahs were male. Brian got the usual teasing questions about what a Scotsman wore under his kilt. "Underwear," was his answer.

"You look wonderful," Lyn told him. The red plaid kilt with knee socks and dark jacket suited him perfectly. "If there was a prize, you'd win it."

"I've already won a prize today," Brian said with a grin.

"Hmm?"

"My mother caved in. I didn't think she would. I always thought she was such a tough lady, but she says I'm tougher. Anyway, she's not going to Boston. She'll commute to a college an hour and a half from here." Proudly he added, "Our family's staying together."

"Brian, that's wonderful!"

"Yeah. She said she couldn't give me up."

Not even for my father, Lyn thought, and was impressed. She was thinking out loud when she said, "So I don't have to worry about Burlap getting in her way in Boston."

"What are you talking about? Burlap's not going to Boston."

"My father said he'd take him if I go."

"But you're not going."

"I think I am. I can't not go, Brian. My father and I have always stuck together. And he's my father."

Brian gave a grudging nod. Of course he understood that, being as close as he was to his own parents. Suddenly he sucked in his breath. "But you can't do that. You can't take Burlap away from me."

"Brian, don't be selfish," she said. "You got everything you wanted. It's not fair if you get our dog, too."

"*Our* dog," he said. "Right, we were sharing him. What happened to that idea?"

The conversation stopped of necessity at the door

of their classroom. Lyn didn't doubt it would be continued.

Later she passed her father standing in the hall wearing a fake mustache, which was the sum total of his Englishman costume. "But Americans have mustaches, too," one of his students was arguing with perfect logic.

"Nothing I can do about that, what?" her father answered with an English accent and a wriggle of his fake mustache.

"Ah, geez!" the student said, and hurried off.

"Right-o." Dad gave a stilted little bow at the student's back.

Being in love with Mrs. Maclean had certainly made him playful, Lyn thought. She smiled over her shoulder at him. His return smile was full of surprise, and she realized he'd gotten used to her being angry at him lately.

All day Lyn seemed to see her friends framed by their importance to her. Jen with her quiet, quirky ways was the one Lyn expected she would become even closer to in high school. In high school, Shelly would be in different classes, following a non-college-bound track, and if Lyn weren't available to call on in an emergency, what would Shelly do? Find another best friend, but maybe one who'd get her into trouble instead of out. Shelly was so impulsive. She needed Lyn to be sensible for her. And Brian! He'd be lonely if Lyn left, and she'd miss him, more maybe than any other friend.

Besides, she belonged in this school district. This was where kids recognized her even without her braid, where she was respected. It would take forever for people to see her that way in a new school, if they ever did. But what could she do, she asked herself on the bus going home. Much as she loved Dora and despite how dear her friends and school were to her, she loved her father more. She could not send him off to Boston without her.

Lyn found Dora vacuuming the living room, a chore she usually avoided. "Want me to do that for you?" Lyn asked as she tossed the Spanish shawl and the comb on the couch.

"I'm almost done. The kennel's empty for a change. So I figured I'd catch up on the housework."

Lyn got it over with fast. "Dora, thanks for saying you'd keep me, but you won't have to. I'm going to Boston with Dad after all."

Dora shut off the noisy vacuum, but kept her eyes on it as she said soberly, "That's what I figured you'd do. Well, I'll miss you." Her jaw twitched. "You know, if you need me—" she began, and then perhaps remembering that she'd said it before, she swallowed and ended lamely, "you let me know." She looked at Lyn with eyes brimming with tenderness, but said only, "I better get this vacuuming done." The whine of the powerful machine ended their exchange.

Still, Lyn was satisfied. Dora did love her. Her eyes showed it and the tone of her voice. She'd welcome Lyn's visits. "I won't let go of her," Lyn vowed to herself. She'd write to Dora, send cards on her birthday and Mother's Day, maintain their attachment every way she could. For Dora, that might be enough.

Dad came home late that night, after Dora had gone to bed. Lyn told him she was going to Boston with him just as he turned on the eleven o'clock news. His smile was beautiful. It went from one ear to the other and made deep creases all over his face.

"Thank you, honey," he said as he hugged her.

She hugged him back. Then she said awkwardly, "I was sort of surprised Mrs. Maclean decided to stay with her husband. I thought you and she were more, you know, that you had a thing for each other."

Dad was less embarrassed to talk about it than she was. "Sylvia's keeping her family intact temporarily for Brian's sake," he said, "at least until she gets her degree. Then we'll see."

"You mean, you may still wind up marrying her?"

"Possibly. We plan to keep in touch and see how it goes. I told you I wasn't rushing into anything, Lyn."

She took a deep breath and said to encourage herself, "I guess it will all work out."

"It will. So long as we stick together, we'll be fine," Dad said confidently. He stroked her hair. "You were right to cut it, Lyn. You look lovely."

"Thanks," she said, and smiled for him and went up to her room.

Burlap was already asleep on the rug next to her bed. She knelt beside him and whispered, "Burpie, you won't mind going with me. You love me enough now, don't you?" Burlap put his head on her knee, and his eyelids crinkled sympathetically as he watched her face. She stroked the soft ear flaps and

150

wondered if *she* wasn't the selfish one to insist Brian give the dog up.

Thursday was T-shirt day. Lyn wore her WOMAN POWER shirt to give her strength. Shelly's shirt was yellow and had a black bee spelling the word HONEY. Jen's had an empty billboard with a FOR RENT sign on it. Brian came to school in jeans and a buttoned-down dress shirt open at the neck.

"Brian, it's T-shirt day," Shelly yelled at him.

"Forgot," he said without concern. He hunched into himself and looked so forbidding all day that even the teachers left him alone.

That night Brian came into the kitchen with Burlap after his walk. "Can I talk to you for a minute, Lyn?"

"Sure."

He looked around while Burlap slurped water from his bowl.

"Dora's comforting a homesick dog in the kennel and Dad's reading in bed," Lyn said. "You can talk."

"Mom met your dad somewhere last night."

"How do you know?"

"I heard my father yelling at her. He didn't know before that your father and she—that there was anything going on between them. I thought it was over." He sounded miserable.

"It seems they're just waiting," Lyn said.

"So what if they get together after all?"

"I don't know. We'll deal with that when it comes, Brian."

"I thought it was settled," Brian said, "and we

knew what was going on. I hate temporary things."

"So do I," she told him.

They looked at each other in silence for a minute. Then Lyn opened the refrigerator and asked, "How about some soda or milk or something?"

"I don't like it," Brian said. "I don't like how it's turning out at all."

He left without responding to her question. Lyn suspected he hadn't even heard it. She knew how he felt. The positives and the negatives kept canceling each other out, and nothing felt good anymore.

The grand finale of Spirit Week was dress-up day on Friday. Lyn put on a shirtwaist and earrings and just a trace of makeup, but left off her heels and took Burlap for his walk wearing her sneakers. Brian stepped out of his house in a gray suit and tie.

"Okay if I walk with you?"

"Sure. You look like a junior executive."

"My father lent me the tie." Shyly Brian added, "You look pretty."

"I feel older. Do you think everything we've been through has aged us?"

"Yeah, at least by a week or two," Brian said sarcastically.

She hesitated about which way to go, and he suggested, "Let's walk to the overpass and watch the cars." It wasn't a destination she would have chosen on her own. They passed the spot where Burlap had been dumped from the pickup truck and left to wait forever for a master who wasn't planning to return. It did seem like a long time ago, maybe because so much had happened in the months between.

They reached the overpass, and Brian leaned on the railing. Lyn propped her elbows up beside him. Below them, cars whizzed by in dits and dots of color. A lady was reading a map in one. In the back of a station wagon, a little boy held up a sign that said, "Hi, I'm Davey." Lyn smiled and waved at him.

"About Burlap," Brian said. "I've done some thinking."

"And?"

He shrugged. "Well, I still think Boston's no place for a big dog like him."

"But you can't keep him, Brian. Your mother'd never let you."

"Dora could board him for me, and I could take care of feeding and walking him and all that," Brian said.

"I don't like the idea of a strange city any more than you, you know."

"Let me finish. . . . So, in some ways, it'd be better for Burlap if you left him here with me. There's plenty of space for him here, whereas in Boston he'd be cooped up somewhere all day until you got home from school."

"But I need him!" she cried. She bit her lip and said woefully, "We're back to getting divorced again, aren't we?"

"It's like that, I guess. And the question is, who gets custody."

Why did families have to break up, Lyn wondered. Why couldn't Dad and Dora have loved each other forever? Losing Burlap, too, would be unbearable.

She needed the big, solid dog in Boston to comfort her for everything she was leaving behind here, so many people she loved, such good times.

A tractor pulling a set of tandem semitrailers passed under the bridge. A piece of broken glass on its roof flashed a message from the sun.

"I always hated division," Lyn said. "I hated it in elementary school, and now I hate it in life."

"Well, anyway," Brian said, doggedly continuing, "the thing is, Burlap might be a little happier here, but you're right. I've come out pretty well—I mean, for the next few years—and you're stuck with all the changes. You need him most, and you'll take good care of him. I know I don't have to worry about that. Besides, you deserve him."

"Oh, Brian," Lyn said, so touched she could barely speak. "You're such a good guy. Thank you. Oh, thank you. What can I say? If I can, I'll bring Burlap back when I come to visit, and I promise I'll ship him back for vacations, like we said."

"Maybe I could visit you in Boston," Brian said.

"Anytime. You won't lose touch with him, you'll see."

"He'll be your dog, though." Brian took a deep breath. "Well, that's the way it goes."

She hugged him and released him quickly. All charged up with emotion, she started talking fast. "I guess Boston will be interesting. I like the country best, but cities are exciting, too. I guess it'll all work out. I mean, for all of us. Somehow. Even Burlap."

Brian squatted until he was nose-to-nose with Burlap, and light brown eyes looked into light brown eyes. "You're some dog, Burpie," he said, "the best I ever met."

"It's possible that it'll work out well, don't you think, Brian?" Lyn asked before climbing aboard the bus in her heels a while later.

"How?" Brian asked.

"Well, I could like Boston, and you could come out okay here."

"I don't think so," he said glumly.

"But it's better to expect it to be all right than wrong," she said. "I mean, why be miserable expecting the worse? Sure, something bad might happen next, but something good might, too. What's interesting is that you never know, right?"

Brian smiled at her, but she couldn't tell whether it was because he thought she was crazy, or whether it meant he liked the idea. At least he was smiling, Lyn thought.